Abraham Cahan

Yekl; a Tale of the New York Ghetto

Abraham Cahan

Yekl; a Tale of the New York Ghetto

ISBN/EAN: 9783337024536

Printed in Europe, USA, Canada, Australia, Japan

Cover: Foto ©Andreas Hilbeck / pixelio.de

More available books at **www.hansebooks.com**

Yekl

A Tale of the New York Ghetto

By

A. Cahan

New York
D. Appleton and Company
1896

CONTENTS.

YEKL.

—

CHAPTER I.

JAKE AND YEKL.

THE operatives of the cloak-shop in which Jake was employed had been idle all the morning. It was after twelve o'clock and the "boss" had not yet returned from Broadway, whither he had betaken himself two or three hours before in quest of work. The little sweltering assemblage—for it was an oppressive day in midsummer — beguiled their suspense variously. A rabbinical-looking man of thirty, who sat with the back of his chair tilted against his sewing machine, was intent upon an English newspaper. Every little while he would remove it from his eyes —showing a dyspeptic face fringed with a

1

thin growth of dark beard—to consult the cumbrous dictionary on his knees. Two young lads, one seated on the frame of the next machine and the other standing, were boasting to one another of their respective intimacies with the leading actors of the Jewish stage. The board of a third machine, in a corner of the same wall, supported an open copy of a socialist magazine in Yiddish, over which a cadaverous young man absorbedly swayed to and fro droning in the Talmudical intonation. A middle-aged operative, with huge red side whiskers, who was perched on the presser's table in the corner opposite, was mending his own coat. While the thick-set presser and all the three women of the shop, occupying the three machines ranged against an adjoining wall, formed an attentive audience to an impromptu lecture upon the comparative merits of Boston and New York by Jake.

He had been speaking for some time. He stood in the middle of the overcrowded stuffy room with his long but well-shaped legs wide apart, his bulky round head aslant, and one of his bared mighty arms akimbo. He spoke in Boston Yiddish, that is to say, in Yiddish more copiously spiced with mutilated English than is the language of the metropolitan Ghetto in which our story lies. He had a deep and rather harsh voice, and his r's could do credit to the thickest Irish brogue.

"When I was in Boston," he went on, with a contemptuous mien intended for the American metropolis, "I knew a *feller*,* so he was a *preticly* friend of John Shullivan's. He is a Christian, that feller is, and yet the two of us lived like brothers. May I be unable to move from this spot if we did not. How, then, would you have it? Like here, in New York, where the Jews are a *lot* of *greenhornsh* and can not speak a word of English? Over there every Jew speaks English like a stream."

---

* English words incorporated in the Yiddish of the characters of this narrative are given in Italics.

"*Say*, Dzake," the presser broke in, "John Sullivan is *tzampion* no longer, is he?"

"Oh, no! Not always is it holiday!" Jake responded, with what he considered a Yankee jerk of his head. "Why, don't you know? Jimmie Corbett *leaked* him, and Jimmie *leaked* Cholly Meetchel, too. *You can betch you' bootsh!* Johnnie could not leak Chollie, *becaush* he is a big *bluffer*, Chollie is," he pursued, his clean-shaven florid face beaming with enthusiasm for his subject, and with pride in the diminutive proper nouns he flaunted. "But Jimmie *pundished* him. *Oh, didn't he knock him out off shight!* He came near making a meat ball of him"—with a chuckle. "He *tzettled* him in three *roynds*. I knew a feller who had seen the fight."

"What is a *rawnd*, Dzake?" the presser inquired.

Jake's answer to the question carried him into a minute exposition of "right-handers," "left-handers," "sending to sleep," "first blood," and other commodities of the fistic

business. He must have treated the subject
rather too scientifically, however, for his female listeners obviously paid more attention
to what he did in the course of the boxing
match, which he had now and then, by way
of illustration, with the thick air of the room,
than to the verbal part of his lecture. Nay,
even the performances of his brawny arms
and magnificent form did not charm them as
much as he thought they did. For a dis-
play of manly force, when connected—even
though in a purely imaginary way—with
acts of violence, has little attraction for a
" daughter of the Ghetto." Much more interest did those arms and form command on
their own merits. Nor was his chubby high-
colored face neglected. True, there was a
suggestion of the bulldog in its make up;
but this effect was lost upon the feminine
portion of Jake's audience, for his features,
illuminated by a pair of eager eyes of a hazel
hue, and shaded by a thick crop of dark hair,
were, after all, rather pleasing than otherwise.
Strongly Semitic naturally, they became still

more so each time they were brightened up
by his good-natured boyish smile. Indeed,
Jake's very nose, which was fleshy and pear-
shaped and decidedly not Jewish (although
not decidedly anything else), seemed to join
the Mosaic faith, and even his shaven upper
lip looked penitent, as soon as that smile of
his made its appearance.

"Nice fun that!" observed the side-whis-
kered man, who had stopped sewing to follow Jake's exhibition. "Fighting — like
drunken moujiks in Russia!"

"Tarrarra-boom-de-ay!" was Jake's merry retort; and for an exclamation mark he
puffed up his cheeks into a balloon, and exploded it by a "*pawnch*" of his formidable
fist.

"Look, I beg you, look at his dog's
tricks!" the other said in disgust.

"Horse's head that you are!" Jake rejoined good-humoredly. "Do you mean to
tell me that a moujik understands how to
fight? A disease he does! He only knows
how to strike like a bear [Jake adapted his

voice and gesticulation to the idea of clumsi-
ness], *an' dot'sh ull!* What does he *care*
where his paw will land, so he strikes. *But*
here one must observe *rulesh* [rules]."

At this point Meester Bernstein—for so
the rabbinical-looking man was usually addressed by his shopmates—looked up from
his dictionary.

"Can't you see?" he interposed, with an
air of assumed gravity as he turned to Jake's
opponent, "America is an educated country,
so they won't even break bones without
grammar. They tear each other's sides according to 'right and left,'* you know."
This was a thrust at Jake's right-handers and
left-handers, which had interfered with Bernstein's reading. "Nevertheless," the latter
proceeded, when the outburst of laughter
which greeted his witticism had subsided,
"I do think that a burly Russian peasant
would, without a bit of grammar, crunch

---

*A term relating to the Hebrew equivalent of
the letter *s*, whose pronunciation depends upon the
right or left position of a mark over it.

the bones of Corbett himself; and he would not *charge* him a cent for it, either."

"*Is dot sho?*" Jake retorted, somewhat nonplussed. "*I betch you* he would not. The peasant would lie bleeding like a hog before he had time to turn around."

"*But* they might kill each other in that way, *ain't it*, Jake?" asked a comely, milk-faced blonde whose name was Fanny. She was celebrated for her lengthy tirades, mostly in a plaintive, nagging strain, and delivered in her quiet, piping voice, and had accordingly been dubbed "The Preacher."

"Oh, that will happen but very seldom," Jake returned rather glumly.

The theatrical pair broke off their boasting match to join in the debate, which soon included all except the socialist; the former two, together with the two girls and the presser, espousing the American cause, while Malke the widow and "De Viskes" sided with Bernstein.

"Let it be as you say," said the leader of the minority, withdrawing from the contest to resume his newspaper. "My grandma's last care it is who can fight best."

"Nice pleasure, *anyhull*," remarked the widow. "*Never min'*, we shall see how it will lie in his head when he has a wife and children to *support*."

Jake colored. "What does a *chicken* know about these things?" he said irascibly.

Bernstein again could not help intervening. "And you, Jake, can not do without 'these things,' can you? Indeed, I do not see how you manage to live without them."

"Don't you like it? I do," Jake declared tartly. "Once I live in America," he pursued, on the defensive, " I want to know that I live in America. *Dot'sh a' kin' a man I am!* One must not be a *greenhorn*. Here a Jew is as good as a Gentile. How, then, would you have it? The way it is in Russia, where a Jew is afraid to stand within four ells of a Christian?"

"Are there no other Christians than '*fighters* in America?" Bernstein objected

with an amused smile. "Why don't you
look for the educated ones ? "

"Do you mean to say the *fighters* are
not *ejecate?* Better than you, *anyhoy*," Jake
said with a Yankee wink, followed by his
Semitic smile. "Here you read the papers,
and yet *I'll betch you* you don't know that
Corbett *findished college."*

"I never read about fighters," Bernstein
replied with a bored gesture, and turned to
his paper.

"Then say that you don't know, and
dot'sh ull!"

Bernstein made no reply. In his heart
Jake respected him, and was now anxious to
vindicate his tastes in the judgment of his
scholarly shopmate and in his own.

"*Alla right*, let it be as you say ; the
fighters are not *ejecate*. No, not a bit !" he
said ironically, continuing to address himself
to Bernstein. "But what will you say to
baseball? All *college boys* and *tony peoplesh*
play it," he concluded triumphantly. Bernstein remained silent, his eyes riveted to his

newspaper. "Ah, you don't answer, *shee ?* " said Jake, feeling put out.

The awkward pause which followed was relieved by one of the playgoers who wanted to know whether it was true that to pitch a ball required more skill than to catch one.

" *Sure !* You must know how to *peetch*," Jake rejoined with the cloud lingering on his brow, as he lukewarmly delivered an imaginary ball.

" And I, for my part, don't see what wisdom there is to it," said the presser with a shrug. " I think I could throw, too."

" He can do everything !" laughingly remarked a girl named Pessé.

" How hard can you hit ? " Jake demanded sarcastically, somewhat warming up to the subject.

" As hard as you at any time."

" *I betch you a dullar to you' ten shent* you can not," Jake answered, and at the same moment he fished out a handful of coin from his trousers pocket and challengingly presented it close to his interlocutor's nose.

2

"There he goes!—betting!" the presser exclaimed, drawing slightly back. "For my part, your *pitzers* and *catzers* may all lie in the earth. A nice entertainment, indeed! Just like little children—playing ball! And yet people say America is a *smart* country. I don't see it."

"'*F caush* you don't, *becaush* you are a bedraggled *greenhorn*, afraid to budge out of Heshter Shtreet." As Jake thus vented his bad humour on his adversary, he cast a glance at Bernstein, as if anxious to attract his attention and to re-engage him in the discussion.

"Look at the Yankee!" the presser shot back.

"More of a one than you, *anyhoy*."

"He thinks that *shaving* one's mustache makes a Yankee!"

Jake turned white with rage.

"'*Pon my vord*, I'll ride into his mug and give such a *shaving* and planing to his pig's snout that he will have to pick up his teeth."

"That's all you are good for."

"Better don't answer him, Jake," said Fanny, intimately.

"Oh, I came near forgetting that he has somebody to take his part!" snapped the presser.

The girl's milky face became a fiery red, and she retorted in vituperative Yiddish from that vocabulary which is the undivided possession of her sex. The presser jerked out an innuendo still more far-reaching than his first. Jake, with bloodshot eyes, leaped at the offender, and catching him by the front of his waistcoat, was aiming one of those bearlike blows which but a short while ago he had decried in the moujik, when Bernstein sprang to his side and tore him away, Pessé placing herself between the two enemies.

"Don't get excited," Bernstein coaxed him.

"Better don't soil your hands," Fanny added.

After a slight pause Bernstein could not

forbear a remark which he had stubbornly repressed while Jake was challenging him to a debate on the education of baseball players: "Look here, Jake; since fighters and baseball men are all educated, then why don't you try to become so ? Instead of *spending* your money on fights, dancing, and things like that, would it not be better if you paid it to a teacher ? "

Jake flew into a fresh passion. "*Never min'* what I do with my money," he said; "I don't steal it from you, do I ? Rejoice that you keep tormenting your books. Much does he know ! Learning, learning, and learning, and still he can not speak English. I don't learn and yet I speak quicker than you ! "

A deep blush of wounded vanity mounted to Bernstein's sallow cheek. "*Ull right, ull right !* " he cut the conversation short, and took up the newspaper.

Another nervous silence fell upon the group. Jake felt wretched. He uttered an English oath, which in his heart he directed against himself as much as against his sedate companion, and fell to frowning upon the leg of a machine.

" Vill you go by Joe to-night ? " asked Fanny in English, speaking in an undertone. Joe was a dancing master. She was sure Jake intended to call at his " academy " that evening, and she put the question only in order to help him out of his sour mood.

" No," said Jake, morosely.

" Vy, to-day is Vensday."

" And without you I don't know it!" he snarled in Yiddish.

The finisher girl blushed deeply and refrained from any response.

" He does look like a *regely* Yankee, doesn't he ? " Pessé whispered to her after a little.

" Go and ask him ! "

" Go and hang yourself together with him ! Such a nasty preacher! Did you ever hear—one dares not say a word to the noblewoman !"

At this juncture the boss, a dwarfish

little Jew, with a vivid pair of eyes and
a shaggy black beard, darted into the
chamber.

"It· is *no used!*" he said with a gesture
of despair. "There is not a stitch of work,
if only for a cure. Look, look how they
have lowered their noses!" he then added
with a triumphant grin. "*Vell,* I shall not
be teasing you, 'Pity living things!' The
expressman is *darn stess.* I would not go
till I saw him *start,* and then I caught
a car. No other *boss* could get a single
jacket even if he fell upon his knees. *Vell,*
do you appreciate it at least? Not much,
ay?"

The presser rushed out of the room and
presently came back laden with bundles of
cut cloth which he threw down on the table.
A wild scramble ensued. The presser
looked on indifferently. The three finisher
women, who had awaited the advent of the
bundles as eagerly as the men, now calmly
put on their hats. They knew that their
part of the work wouldn't come before three

o'clock, and so, overjoyed by the certainty of
employment for at least another day or two,
they departed till that hour.

"Look at the rush they are making!
Just like the locusts of Egypt!" the boss
cried half sternly and half with self-compla-
cent humour, as he shielded the treasure with
both his arms from all except " De Viskes "
and Jake—the two being what is called in
sweat-shop parlance, " *chance-mentshen*," i. e.,
favorites. " Don't be snatching and catching like that," the boss went on. "You
may burn your fingers. Go to your machines, I say! The soup will be served
in separate plates. Never fear, it won't get
cold."

The hands at last desisted gingerly, Jake
and the whiskered operator carrying off
two of the largest bundles. The others
went to their machines empty-handed and
remained seated, their hungry glances riveted to the booty, until they, too, were provided.

The little boss distributed the bundles

with dignified deliberation. In point of fact,
he was no less impatient to have the work
started than any of his employees. But in
him the feeling was overridden by a kind of
malicious pleasure which he took in their
eagerness and in the demonstration of his
power over the men, some of whom he
knew to have enjoyed a more comfort-
able past than himself. The machines of
Jake and " De Viskes " led off in a duet,
which presently became a trio, and in another few minutes the floor was fairly dancing to the ear-piercing discords of the whole
frantic sextet.

In the excitement of the scene called
forth by the appearance of the bundles,
Jake's gloomy mood had melted away.
Nevertheless, while his machine was deliv-
ering its first shrill staccatos, his heart recited
a vow : "As soon as I get my pay I shall
call on the installment .man and give him a
deposit for a ticket." The prospective ticket
was to be for a passage across the Atlantic
from Hamburg to New York. And as the

notion of it passed through Jake's mind it
evoked there the image of a dark-eyed
young woman with a babe in her lap.
However, as the sewing machine throbbed
and writhed under Jake's lusty kicks, it
seemed to be swiftly carrying him away from
the apparition which had the effect of reced-
ing, as a wayside object does from the pas-
senger of a flying train, until it lost itself in
a misty distance, other visions emerging in
its place.

It was some three years before the opening of this story that Jake had last beheld
that very image in the flesh. But then at
that period of his life he had not even suspected the existence of a name like Jake, being known to himself and to all Povodye—a
town in northwestern Russia—as Yekl or
Yekelé.

It was not as a deserter from military
service that he had shaken off the dust of
that town where he had passed the first
twenty-two years of his life. As the only
son of aged parents he had been exempt

from the duty of bearing arms. Jake may
have forgotten it, but his mother still frequently recurs to the day when he came
rushing home, panting for breath, with the
" red certificate " assuring his immunity in
his hand. She nearly fainted for happiness.
And when, stroking his dishevelled sidelocks
with her bony hand and feasting her eye on
his chubby face, she whispered, " My recov-
ered child ! God be blessed for his mercy ! "
there was a joyous tear in his eye as well as
in hers. Well does she remember how she
gently spat on his forehead three times to
avert the effect of a possible evil eye on her
" flourishing tree of a boy," and how his father standing by made merry over what he
called her crazy womanish tricks, and said
she had better fetch some brandy in honour
of the glad event.

But if Yekl was averse to wearing a soldier's uniform on his own person he was
none the less fond of seeing it on others.
His ruling passion, even after he had become a husband and a father, was to watch

the soldiers drilling on the square in front of the whitewashed barracks near which stood his father's smithy. From a cheder * boy he showed a knack at placing himself on terms of familiarity with the Jewish members of the local regiment, whose uniforms struck terror into the hearts of his schoolmates. He would often play truant to attend a military parade ; no lad in town knew so many Russian words or was as well versed in army terminology as Yekelé " Beril the blacksmith's ;" and after he had left cheder, while working his father's bellows, Yekl would vary synagogue airs with martial song.

Three years had passed since Yekl had for the last time set his eyes on the whitewashed barracks and on his father's rickety smithy, which, for reasons indirectly connected with the Government's redoubled discrimination against the sons of Israel, had become inadequate to support two families ;

---

* A school where Jewish children are instructed in the Old Testament or the Talmud.

three years since that beautiful summer
morning when he had mounted the spacious
kibitka which was to carry him to the fron-
tier-bound train; since, hurried by the driver,
he had leaned out of the wagon to kiss his
half-year old son good-bye amid the heartrending lamentations of his wife, the tremulous "Go in good health!" of his father, and
the startled screams of the neighbours who
rushed to the relief of his fainting mother.
The broken Russian learned among the Povodye soldiers he had exchanged for English of a corresponding quality, and the bellows for a sewing machine—a change of
weapons in the battle of life which had been
brought about both by Yekl's tender religious feelings and robust legs. He had been
shocked by the very notion of seeking employment at his old trade in a city where it
is in the hands of Christians, and conse-
quently involves a violation of the Mosaic
Sabbath. On the other hand, his legs had
been thought by his early American advisers
eminently fitted for the treadle. Unlike

New York, the Jewish sweat-shops of Boston keep in line, as a rule, with the Christian factories in observing Sunday as the only day of rest. There is, however, even in Boston a lingering minority of bosses—more particularly in the " pants "-making branch— who abide by the Sabbath of their fathers. Accordingly, it was under one of these that Yekl had first been initiated into the sweat-shop world.

Subsequently Jake, following numerous examples, had given up " pants " for the more remunerative cloaks, and having rapidly attained skill in his new trade he had moved to New York, the centre of the cloak-making industry.

Soon after his arrival in Boston his religious scruples had followed in the wake of his former first name ; and if he was still free from work on Saturdays he found many another way of " desecrating the Sabbath."

Three years had intervened since he had first set foot on American soil, and the thought of ever having been a Yekl would bring to Jake's lips a smile of patronizing commiseration for his former self. As to his Russian family name, which was Podkovnik, Jake's friends had such rare use for it that by mere negligence it had been left intact.

CHAPTER II.

It was after seven in the evening when
Jake finished his last jacket. Some of the
operators had laid down their work before,
while others cast an envious glance on him
as he was dressing to leave, and fell to their
machines with reluctantly redoubled energy.
Fanny was a week worker and her time had
been up at seven; but on this occasion her
toilet had taken an uncommonly long time,
and she was not ready until Jake got up
from his chair. Then she left the room
rather suddenly and with a demonstrative
" Good-night all ! "

When Jake reached the street he found
her on the sidewalk, making a pretense of

brushing one of her sleeves with the cuff of the other.

"So kvick?" she asked, raising her head in feigned surprise.

"You cull dot kvick?" he returned grimly. "Good-bye!"

"Say, ain't you goin' to dance to-night, really?" she queried shamefacedly.

"I tol' you I vouldn't."

"What does *she* want of me?" he complained to himself proceeding on his way. He grew conscious of his low spirits, and, tracing them with some effort to their source, he became gloomier still. "No more fun for me!" he decided. "I shall get them over here and begin a new life."

After supper, which he had taken, as usual, at his lodgings, he went out for a walk. He was firmly determined to keep himself from visiting Joe Peltner's dancing academy, and accordingly he took a direction opposite to Suffolk Street, where that establishment was situated. Having passed a few blocks, however, his feet, contrary to

his will, turned into a side street and thence
into one leading to Suffolk. " I shall only
drop in to tell Joe that I can not sell any of
his ball tickets, and return them," he at-
tempted to deceive his own conscience.
Hailing this pretext with delight he quickened his pace as much as the overcrowded
sidewalks would allow.

He had to pick and nudge his way
through dense swarms of bedraggled half-
naked humanity ; past garbage barrels rear-
ing their overflowing contents in sickening
piles, and lining the streets in malicious suggestion of rows of trees ; underneath tiers
and tiers of fire escapes, barricaded and fes-
tooned with mattresses, pillows, and feather-
beds not yet gathered in for the night. The
pent-in sultry atmosphere was laden with
nausea and pierced with a discordant and, as
it were, plaintive buzz. Supper had been
despatched in a hurry, and the teeming popu-
lations of the cyclopic tenement houses were
out in full force " for fresh air," as even these
people will say in mental quotation marks.

3

Suffolk Street is in the very thick of the battle for breath. For it lies in the heart of that part of the East Side which has within the last two or three decades become the Ghetto of the American metropolis, and, indeed, the metropolis of the Ghettos of the world. It is one of the most densely populated spots on the face of the earth—a seething human sea fed by streams, streamlets, and rills of immigration flowing from all the Yiddish-speaking centres of Europe. Hardly a block but shelters Jews from every nook and corner of Russia, Poland, Galicia, Hungary, Roumania; Lithuanian Jews, Volhynian Jews, south Russian Jews, Bessarabian Jews; Jews crowded out of the "pale of Jewish settlement"; Russified Jews expelled from Moscow, St. Petersburg, Kieff, or Saratoff; Jewish runaways from justice; Jewish refugees from crying political and economical injustice; people torn from a hard-gained foothold in life and from deep-rooted attachments by the caprice of intolerance or the wiles of demagoguery—innocent scapegoats of a guilty Government for its outraged populace to misspend its blind fury upon; students shut out of the Russian universities, and come to these shores in quest of learning; artisans, merchants, teachers, rabbis, artists, beggars—all come in search of fortune. Nor is there a tenement house but harbours in its bosom specimens of all the whimsical metamorphoses wrought upon the children of Israel of the great modern exodus by the vicissitudes of life in this their Promised Land of to-day. You find there Jews born to plenty, whom the new conditions have delivered up to the clutches of penury; Jews reared in the straits of need, who have here risen to prosperity; good people morally degraded in the struggle for success amid an unwonted environment; moral outcasts lifted from the mire, purified, and imbued with self-respect; educated men and women with their intellectual polish tarnished in the inclement weather of adversity; ignorant sons of toil grown enlightened—in fine, people with all sorts of antecedents, tastes, habits, inclinations, and speaking all sorts of subdialects of the same jargon, thrown pellmell into one social caldron—a human hodgepodge with its component parts changed but not yet fused into one homogeneous whole.

And so the "stoops," sidewalks, and pavements of Suffolk Street were thronged with panting, chattering, or frisking multitudes. In one spot the scene received a kind of weird picturesqueness from children dancing on the pavement to the strident music hurled out into the tumultuous din from a row of the open and brightly illuminated windows of what appeared to be a new tenement house. Some of the young women on the sidewalk opposite raised a longing eye to these windows, for floating by through the dazzling light within were young women like themselves with masculine arms round their waists.

As the spectacle caught Jake's eye his heart gave a leap. He violently pushed his way through the waltzing swarm, and dived into the half-dark corridor of the house whence the music issued. Presently he found himself on the threshold and in the overpowering air of a spacious oblong chamber, alive with a damp-haired, dishevelled, reeking crowd—an uproarious human vortex, whirling to the squeaky notes of a violin and the thumping of a piano. The room was, judging by its untidy, once-whitewashed walls and the uncouth wooden pillars supporting its bare ceiling, more accustomed to the whir of sewing machines than to the noises which filled it at the present moment. It took up the whole of the first floor of a five-story house built for large sweat-shops, and until recently it had served its original purpose as faithfully as the four upper floors, which were still the daily scenes of feverish industry. At the further end of the room there was now a marble soda fountain in charge of an unkempt boy. A stocky young man with a black entanglement of coarse curly hair was bustling about among the dancers. Now and then he

would pause with his eyes bent upon some
two pairs of feet, and fall to clapping time
and drawling out in a preoccupied sing-
song: "Von, two, tree! Leeft you' feet!
Don' so kvick—sloy, sloy! Von, two, tree,
von, two, tree!" This was Professor Peltner himself, whose curly hair, by the way,
had more to do with the success of his institution than his stumpy legs, which, according to the unanimous dictum of his male pupils, moved about "like a *regely* pair of
bears."

The throng showed but a very scant
sprinkling of plump cheeks and shapely figures in a multitude of haggard faces and flac-
cid forms. Nearly all were in their work-a-
day clothes, very few of the men sporting a
wilted white shirt front. And while the
general effect of the kaleidoscope was one of
boisterous hilarity, many of the individual
couples somehow had the air of being engaged in hard toil rather than as if they were
dancing for amusement. The faces of some
of these bore a wondering martyrlike ex-

pression, as who should say, " What have
we done to be knocked about in this manner ? "   For the rest, there were all sorts of
attitudes and miens in the whirling crowd.
One young fellow, for example, seemed to
be threatening vengeance to the ceiling,
while his partner was all but exultantly exclaiming : " Lord of the universe! What a
world this be!" Another maiden looked as
if she kept murmuring, " You don't say!"
whereas her cavalier mutely ejaculated,
" Glad to try my best, your noble birth!"—
after the fashion of a Russian soldier.

The prevailing stature of the assemblage
was rather below medium. This does not
include the dozen or two of undergrown
lasses of fourteen or thirteen who had come
surreptitiously, and—to allay the suspicion
of their mothers—in their white aprons.
They accordingly had only these articles to
check at the hat box, and hence the nick-
name of " apron-check ladies," by which this
truant contingent was known at Joe's academy. So that as Jake now stood in the

doorway with an orphaned collar button glistening out of the band of his collarless shirt front and an affected expression of *ennui* overshadowing his face, his strapping figure towered over the circling throng before him. He was immediately noticed and became the target for hellos, smiles, winks, and all manner of pleasantry : "Vot you stand like dot ? You vont to loin dantz?" or "You a detectiff?" or "You vont a job?" or, again, "Is it hot anawff for you ?" To all of which Jake returned an invariable "Yep!" each time resuming his bored mien.

As he thus gazed at the dancers, a feeling of envy came over him. "Look at them!" he said to himself begrudgingly. "How merry they are! Such *shnoozes*, they can hardly set a foot well, and yet they are free, while I am a married man. But wait till you get married, too," he prospectively avenged himself on Joe's pupils; "we shall see how you will then dance and jump!"

Presently a wave of Joe's hand brought

the music and the trampling to a pause.
The girls at once took their seats on the
"ladies' bench," while the bulk of the men
retired to the side reserved for "gents only."
Several apparent post-graduates nonchalant-
ly overstepped the boundary line, and, nothing daunted by the professor's repeated
"Zents to de right an' ladess to the left!"
unrestrainedly kept their girls chuckling.
At all events, Joe soon desisted, his attention being diverted by the soda department
of his business. "Sawda!" he sang out.
"Ull kin's! Sam, you ought ashamed you'-
selv; vy don'tz you treat you' lada?"

In the meantime Jake was the centre of
a growing bevy of both sexes. He refused
to unbend and to enter into their facetious
mood, and his morose air became the topic
of their persiflage.

By-and-bye Joe came scuttling up to his
side. "Goot-evenig, Dzake!" he greeted
him; "I didn't seen you at ull! Say, Dzake,
I'll take care dis site an' you take care dot
site—ull right?"

"Alla right!" Jake responded gruffly. "Gentsh, getch you partnesh, hawrry up!" he commanded in another instant.

The sentence was echoed by the dancing master, who then blew on his whistle a prolonged shrill warble, and once again the floor was set straining under some two hundred pounding, gliding, or scraping feet.

"Don' bee 'fraid. Gu right aheat an' getch you partner!" Jake went on yelling right and left. "Don' be 'shamed, Mish Cohen. Dansh mit dot gentlemarn!" he said, as he unceremoniously encircled Miss Cohen's waist with "dot gentlemarn's" arm. "Cholly! vot's de madder mitch *you*? You do hop like a Cossack, as true as I am a Jew," he added, indulging in a momentary lapse into Yiddish. English was the official language of the academy, where it was broken and mispronounced in as many different ways as there were Yiddish dialects represented in that institution. "Dot'sh de vay, look!" With which Jake seized from Charley a lanky fourteen-year-old Miss Jacobs, and proceeded to set an example of correct waltzing, much to the unconcealed delight of the girl, who let her head rest on his breast with an air of reverential gratitude and bliss, and to the embarrassment of her cavalier, who looked at the evolutions of Jake's feet without seeing.

Presently Jake was beckoned away to a corner by Joe, whereupon Miss Jacobs, looking daggers at the little professor, sulked off to a distant seat.

" Dzake, do me a faver; hask Mamic to gib dot feller a couple a dantzes," Joe said imploringly, pointing to an ungainly young man who was timidly viewing the pandemonium-like spectacle from the further end of the " gent's bench." " I hasked 'er myself, but se don' vonted. He's a beesness man, you 'destan', an' he kan a lot o' fellers an' I vonted make him satetzfiet."

" Dot monkey ? " said Jake. " Vot you talkin' aboyt ! She vouldn't lishn to me neider, honesht."

" Say dot you don' vonted and dot's ull."

"Alla right; I'm goin' to ashk her, but I know it vouldn't be of naw used."

"Never min', you hask 'er foist. You knaw se vouldn't refuse *you!*" Joe urged, with a knowing grin.

"Hoy much vill you bet she will refushe shaw?" Jake rejoined with insincere vehemence, as he whipped out a handful of change.

"Vot kin' foon a man you are! Ulleways' like to bet!" said Joe, deprecatingly. "'F cuss it depend mit vot kin' a mout' you vill hask, you 'destan'?"

"By gum, Jaw! Vot you take me for? Ven I shay I ashk, I ashk. You knaw I don' like no monkey beeshnesh. Ven I promish anytink I do it shquare, dot'sh a kin' a man *I* am!" And once more protesting his firm conviction that Mamie would disregard his request, he started to prove that she would not.

He had to traverse nearly the entire length of the hall, and, notwithstanding that he was compelled to steer clear of the dancers, he contrived to effect the passage at the swellest of his gaits, which means that he jauntily bobbed and lurched, after the manner of a blacksmith tugging at the bellows, and held up his enormous bullet head as if he were bidding defiance to the whole world. Finally he paused in front of a girl with a superabundance of pitch-black side bangs and with a pert, ill natured, pretty face of the most strikingly Semitic cast in the whole gathering. She looked twenty-three or more, was inclined to plumpness, and her shrewd deep dark eyes gleamed out of a warm gipsy complexion. Jake found her seated in a fatigued attitude on a chair near the piano.

"Good-evenig, Mamie!" he said, bowing with mock gallantry.

" Rats!"

" Shay, Mamie, give dot feller a tvisht, vill you?"

" Dot slob again? Joe must tink if you ask me I'll get scared, ain't it? Go and tell him he is too fresh," she said with a con-

temptuous grimace. Like the majority of
the girls of the academy, Mamie's English
was a much nearer approach to a justifica-
tion of its name than the gibberish spoken
by the men.

Jake felt routed; but he put a bold face on
it and broke out with studied resentment :

"Vot you kickin' aboyt, anyhoy? Jaw
don' mean notin' at ull. If you don'
vonted never min', an' dot'sh ull. It don'
cut a figger, shee?" And he feignedly
turned to go.

"Look how kvick he gets excited !" she
said, surrenderingly.

" I ain't get ekshitet at ull; but vot'sh de
used a makin' monkey beesnesh?" he retorted with triumphant acerbity.

"You are a monkey you'self," she returned with a playful pout.

The compliment was acknowledged by
one of Jake's blandest grins.

"An' you are a monkey from monkey-
land," he said. "Vill you dansh mit dot
feller?"

" Rats ! Vot vill you give me ? "

" Vot should I give you ? " he asked impatiently.

" Vill you treat ? "

" Treat ? Ger-rr oyt ! " he replied with a sweeping kick at space.

" Den I von't dance."

" Alla right. I'll treat you mit a coupel a waltch."

" Is dot so ? You must really tink I am swooning to dance vit you," she said, dividing the remark between both jargons.

" Look at her, look ! she is a *regely* getzke * : one must take off one's cap to speak to her. Don't you always say you like to *dansh* with me *becush* I am a good *dansher ?* "

" You must tink you are a peach of a dancer, ain' it ? Bennie can dance a —— sight better dan you," she recurred to her English.

---

* A crucifix.

"Alla right!" he said tartly. "So you don' vonted?"

"O sugar! He is gettin' mad again. Vell, who is de getzke, me or you? All right, I'll dance vid de slob. But it's only becuss you ask me, mind you!" she added fawningly.

"Dot'sh alla right!" he rejoined, with an affectation of gravity, concealing his triumph. "But you makin' too much fush. I like to shpeak plain, shee? Dot'sh a kin' a man *I* am."

The next two waltzes Mamie danced with the ungainly novice, taking exaggerated pains with him. Then came a lancers, Joe calling out the successive movements huckster fashion. His command was followed by less than half of the class, however, for the greater part preferred to avail themselves of the same music for waltzing. Jake was bent upon giving Mamie what he called a "sholid good time"; and, as she shared his view that a square or fancy dance was as flimsy an affair as a stick of candy, they joined or, rather, led the seceding majority. They spun along with all-forgetful gusto; every little while he lifted her on his powerful arm and gave her a " mill," he yelping and she squeaking for sheer ecstasy, as he did so; and throughout the performance his face and his whole figure seemed to be exclaiming, " Dot'sh a kin' a man *I* am ! "

Several waifs stood in a cluster admiring or begrudging the antics of the star couple. Among these was lanky Miss Jacobs and Fanny the Preacher, who had shortly before made her appearance in the hall, and now stood pale and forlorn by the " apron-check " girl's side.

" Look at the way she is stickin' to him ! " the little girl observed with envious venom, her gaze riveted to Mamie, whose shapely head was at this moment reclining on Jake's shoulders, with her eyes half shut, as if melting in a transport of bliss.

Fanny felt cut to the quick.

" You are, jealous, ain't you ? " she jerked out.

4

"Who, me? Vy should I be jealous?"
Miss Jacobs protested, colouring. "On my
part let them both go to ——. *You* must
be jealous. Here, here! See how your
eyes are creeping out looking! Here,
here!" she teased her offender in Yiddish,
poking her little finger at her as she spoke.

"Will you shut your scurvy mouth, little
piece of ugliness, you? Such a piggish
apron check!" poor Fanny burst out under
breath, tears starting to her eyes.

"Such a nasty little runt!" another girl
chimed in.

"Such a little cricket already knows
what 'jealous' is!" a third of the bystanders
put in. "You had better go home or your
mamma will give you a spanking." Whereat the little cricket made a retort, which had
better be left unrecorded.

"To think of a bit of a flea like that having so much *cheek!* Here is America for
you!"

"America for a country and '*dod'll do*'
[that'll do] for a language!" observed one of

the young men of the group, indulging one of the stereotype jokes of the Ghetto.

The passage at arms drew Jake's attention to the little knot of spectators, and his eye fell on Fanny. Whereupon he summarily relinquished his partner on the floor, and advanced toward his shopmate, who, seeing him approach, hastened to retreat to the girls' bench, where she remained scated with a drooping head.

" Hello, Fanny ! " he shouted briskly, coming up in front of her.

" Hello ! " she returned rigidly, her eyes fixed on the dirty floor.

" Come, give ush a tvisht, vill you ? "

" But you ain't goin' by Joe to-night ! " she answered, with a withering curl of her lip, her glance still on the ground. " Go to your lady, she'll be mad atch you."

" I didn't vonted to gu here, honesht, Fanny. I o'ly come to tell Jaw shometin', an' dot'sh ull," he said guiltily.

" Why should you apologize ? " she addressed the tip of her shoe in her mother tongue. "As if he was obliged to apologize to me! *For my part* you can *dance* with her day and night. *Vot do I care?* As if I *cared!* I have only come to see what a *bluffer* you are. Do you think I am a *fool?* As *smart* as your Mamie, *anyvay.* As if I had not known he wanted to make me stay at home! What are you afraid of? Am I in your way then? As if I was in his way! What business have I to be in your way? Who is in your way?"

While she was thus speaking in her voluble, querulous, harassing manner, Jake stood with his hands in his trousers' pockets, in an attitude of mock attention. Then, suddenly losing patience, he said:

"*Dot'sh alla right!* You will finish your sermon afterward. And in the meantime *lesh have a valtz* from the land of *valtzes!*" With which he forcibly dragged her off her seat, catching her round the waist.

"But I don't need it, I don't wish it! Go to your Mamie!" she protested, strug-

gling. "I tell you I don't need it, I don't
——" The rest of the sentence was choked
off by her violent breathing; for by this time
she was spinning with Jake like a top.
After another moment's pretense at struggling to free herself she succumbed, and presently clung to her partner, the picture of triumph and beatitude.

Meanwhile Mamie had walked up to
Joe's side, and without much difficulty
caused him to abandon the lancers party to
themselves, and to resume with her the waltz
which Jake had so abruptly broken off.

In the course of the following intermis-
sion she diplomatically seated herself beside
her rival, and paraded her tranquillity of
mind by accosting her with a question on
shop matters. Fanny was not blind to the
manœuvre, but her exultation was all the
greater for it, and she participated in the ensuing conversation with exuberant geniality.

By-and-bye they were joined by Jake.

"Vell, vill you treat, Jake?" said Mamie.

"Vot you vant, a kish?" he replied, putting his offer in action as well as in language.

Mamie slapped his arm.

"May the Angel of Death kiss you!" said her lips in Yiddish. "Try again!" her glowing face overruled them in a dialect of its own.

Fanny laughed.

"Once I am *treating*, both *ladas* must be *treated* alike, *ain' it?*" remarked the gallant, and again he proved himself as good as his word, although Fanny struggled with greater energy and ostensibly with more real indignation.

"But vy don't you treat, you stingy loafer you?"

"Vot elsh you vant? A peench?" He was again on the point of suiting the action to the word, but Mamie contrived to repay the pinch before she had received it, and added a generous piece of profanity into the bargain. Whereupon tnere ensued a scuffle of a character which defies description in more senses than one.

Nevertheless Jake marched his two " ladas" up to the marble fountain, and regaled them with two cents' worth of soda each.

An hour or so later, when Jake got out into the street, his breast pocket was loaded with a fresh batch of " Professor Peltner's Grand Annual Ball" tickets, and his two arms—with Mamie and Fanny respectively.

" As soon as I get my wages I'll call on the installment agent and give him a deposit for a steamship ticket," presently glimmered through his mind, as he adjusted his hold upon the two girls, snugly gathering them to his sides.

CHAPTER III.

JAKE had never even vaguely abandoned the idea of supplying his wife and child with the means of coming to join him. He was more or less prompt in remitting her monthly allowance of ten rubles, and the visit to the draft and passage office had become part of the routine of his life. It had the invariable effect of arousing his dormant scruples, and he hardly ever left the office without ascertaining the price of a steerage voyage from Hamburg to New York. But no sooner did he emerge from the dingy basement into the noisy scenes of Essex Street, than he would consciously let his mind wander off to other topics.

Formerly, during the early part of his so-
journ in Boston, his landing place, where
some of his townsfolk resided and where he
had passed his first two years in America, he
used to mention his Gitl and his Yosselé so
frequently and so enthusiastically, that some
wags among the Hanover Street tailors
would sing "Yekl and wife and the baby" to
the tune of Molly and I and the Baby.
In the natural course of things, however,
these retrospective effusions gradually became far between, and since he had shifted
his abode to New York he carefully avoided
all reference to his antecedents. The Jewish
quarter of the metropolis, which is a vast and
compact city within a city, offers its denizens
incomparably fewer chances of contact with
the English-speaking portion of the popula-
tion than any of the three separate Ghettos
of Boston. As a consequence, since Jake's
advent to New York his passion for American sport had considerably cooled off. And,
to make up for this, his enthusiastic nature
before long found vent in dancing and in a

general life of gallantry. His proved knack
with the gentle sex had turned his head and
now cost him all his leisure time. Still, he
would occasionally attend some variety show
in which boxing was the main drawing card,
and somehow managed to keep track of the
salient events of the sporting world generally. Judging from his unstaid habits and
happy-go-lucky abandon to the pleasures of
life, his present associates took it for granted
that he was single, and instead of twitting
him with the feigned assumption that he had
deserted a family—a piece of burlesque as
old as the Ghetto—they would quiz him as
to which of his girls he was " dead struck "
on, and as to the day fixed for the wedding.
On more than one such occasion he had on
the tip of his tongue the seemingly jocular
question, " How do you know I am not married already ? " But he never let the sentence cross his lips, and would, instead, observe facetiously that he was not " shtruck
on nu goil," and that he was dead struck on
all of them in " whulshale." " I hate retail

beesnesh, shee ?. Dot'sh a' kin' a man *I*
am !" One day, in the course of an intimate
conversation with Joe, Jake, dropping into a
philosophical mood, remarked :

"It's something like a baker, *ain't it?*
The more *cakes* he has the less he likes
them. You and I have a *lot* of girls ; that's
why we don't *care* for any one of them."

But if his attachment for the girls of his
acquaintance collectively was not coupled
with a quivering of his heart for any individual Mamie, or Fanny, or Sarah, it did not,
on the other hand, preclude a certain lingering tenderness for his wife. But then his
wife, had long since ceased to be what she
had been of yore. From a reality she had
gradually become transmuted into a fancy.
During the three years since he had set foot
on the soil, where a "shister * becomes a
mister and a mister a shister," he had lived so
much more than three years—so much more,
in fact, than in all the twenty-two years

---

* Yiddish for shoemaker.

of his previous life—that his Russian past
appeared to him a dream and his wife and
child, together with his former self, fellow-
characters in a charming tale, which he was
neither willing to banish from his memory
nor able to reconcile with the actualities of
his American present. The question of how
to effect this reconciliation, and of causing
Gitl and little Yosselé to step out of the
thickening haze of reminiscence and to take
their stand by his side as living parts of his
daily life, was a fretful subject from the con-
sideration of which he cowardly shrank. He
wished he could both import his family and
continue his present mode of life. At the
bottom of his soul he wondered why this
should not be feasible. But he knew that it
was not, and his heart would sink at the notion of forfeiting the lion's share of attentions for which he came in at the hands of
those who lionized him. Moreover, how
will he look people in the face in view of the
lie he has been acting? He longed for an
interminable respite. But as sooner or later

the minds of his acquaintances were bound
to become disabused, and he would have to
face it all out anyway, he was many a time
on the point of making a clean breast of it,
and failed to do so for a mere lack of nerve,
each time letting himself off on the plea that
a week or two before his wife's arrival would
be a more auspicious occasion for the dis-
closure.

Neither Jake nor his wife nor his parents
could write even Yiddish, although both he
and his old father read fluently the punctu-
ated Hebrew of the Old Testament or the
Prayer-book. Their correspondence had
therefore to be carried on by proxy, and, as
a consequence, at longer intervals than would
have been the case otherwise. The missives
which he received differed materially in
length, style, and degree of illiteracy as well
as in point of penmanship; but they all
agreed in containing glowing encomiums of
little Yosselé, exhorting Yekl not to stray
from the path of righteousness, and reproach-
fully asking whether he ever meant to send

the ticket. The latter point had an exasper-
ating effect on Jake. There were times,
however, when it would touch his heart and
elicit from him his threadbare vow to send
the ticket at once. But then he never had
money enough to redeem it. And, to tell
the truth, at the bottom of his heart he was
at such moments rather glad of his poverty.
At all events, the man who wrote Jake's letters had a standing order to reply in the
sharpest terms at his command that Yekl
did not spend his money on drink; that
America was not the land they took it for,
where one could "scoop gold by the skirt-
ful;" that Gitl need not fear lest he meant to
desert her, and that as soon as he had saved
enough to pay her way and to set up a de-
cent establishment she would be sure to get
the ticket.

Jake's scribe was an old Jew who kept a
little stand on Pitt Street, which is one of
the thoroughfares and market places of the
Galician quarter of the Ghetto, and where
Jake was unlikely to come upon any people

of his acquaintance. The old man scraped together his livelihood by selling Yiddish newspapers and cigarettes, and writing letters for a charge varying, according to the length of the epistle, from five to ten cents. Each time Jake received a letter he would take it to the Galician, who would first read it to him (for an extra remuneration of one cent) and then proceed to pen five cents' worth of rhetoric, which might have been printed and forwarded one copy at a time for all the additions or alterations Jake ever caused to be made in it.

["What else shall I write?" the old man would ask his patron, after having written and read aloud the first dozen lines, which Jake had come to know by heart.]

" How do *I* know?" Jake would respond. It is you who can write; so you ought to understand what else to write."

And the scribe would go on to write what he had written on almost every previous occasion. Jake would keep the letter in his pocket until he had spare United

States money enough to convert into ten
rubles, and then he would betake himself
to the draft office and have the amount, together with the well-crumpled epistle, forwarded to Povodye.

And so it went month in and month
out.

The first letter which reached Jake after
the scene at Joe Peltner's dancing academy
came so unusually close upon its predecessor
that he received it from his landlady's hand
with a throb of misgiving. He had always
laboured under the presentiment that some
unknown enemies—for he had none that he
could name—would some day discover his
wife's address and anonymously represent
him to her as contemplating another marriage, in order to bring Gitl down upon him
unawares. His first thought accordingly
was that this letter was the outcome of such
a conspiracy. "Or maybe there is some
death in the family?" he next reflected, half
with terror and half with a feeling almost
amounting to reassurance.

When the cigarette vender unfolded the letter he found it to be of such unusual length that he stipulated an additional cent for the reading of it.

"*Alla right*, hurry up now!" Jake said, grinding his teeth on a mumbled English oath.

"*Righd evay! Righd evay!*" the old fellow returned jubilantly, as he hastily adjusted his spectacles and addressed himself to his task.

The letter had evidently been penned by some one laying claim to Hebrew scholarship and ambitious to impress the New World with it ; for it was quite replete with poetic digressions, strained and twisted to suit some quotation from the Bible. And what with this unstinted verbosity, which was Greek to Jake, one or two interruptions by the old man's customers, and interpretations necessitated by difference of dialect, a quarter of an hour had elapsed before the scribe realized the trend of what he was reading.

5

Then he suddenly gave a start, as if
shocked.

"Vot'sh a madder? Vot'sh a madder?"

"*Vot's der madder?* What should be
the *madder?* Wait—a—I don't know what
I can do"—he halted in perplexity.

"Any bad news?" Jake inquired, turning
pale. "Speak out!"

"Speak out! It is all very well for you
to say 'speak out.' You forget that one is a
piece of Jew," he faltered, hinting at the orthodox custom which enjoins a child of Israel from being the messenger of sad tidings.

"Don't *bodder* a head!" Jake shouted
savagely. "I have paid you, haven't I?"

"*Say*, young man, you need not be so
angry," the other said, resentfully. "Half of
the letter I have read, have I not? so I shall
refund you one cent and leave me in peace."
He took to fumbling in his pockets for the
coin, with apparent reluctance.

"Tell me what is the matter," Jake en-
treated, with clinched fists. "Is anybody
dead? Do tell me now."

" *Vell,* since you know it already, I may as well tell you," said the scribe cunningly, glad to retain the cent and Jake's patronage. " It is your father who has been freed; may he have a bright paradise."

" Ha?" Jake asked aghast, with a wide gape.

The Galician resumed the reading in solemn, doleful accents. The melancholy passage was followed by a jeremiade upon the penniless condition of the family and Jake's duty to send the ticket without further procrastination. As to his mother, she preferred the Povodye graveyard to a watery sepulchre, and hoped that her beloved and only son, the apple of her eye, whom she had been awake nights to bring up to manhood, and so forth, would not forget her.

" So now they will be here for sure, and there can be no more delay!" was Jake's first distinct thought. " Poor father!" he inwardly exclaimed the next moment, with deep anguish. His native home came back to him with a vividness which it had not had in his mind for a long time.

"Was he an old man?" the scribe queried sympathetically.

"About seventy," Jake answered, bursting into tears.

"Seventy? Then he had lived to a good old age. May no one depart younger," the old man observed, by way of "consoling the bereaved."

As Jake's tears instantly ran dry he fell to wringing his hands and moaning.

"Good-night!" he presently said, taking leave. "I'll see you to-morrow, if God be pleased."

"Good-night!" the scribe returned with heartfelt condolence.

As he was directing his steps to his lodgings Jake wondered why he did not weep. He felt that this was the proper thing for a man in his situation to do, and he endeavoured to inspire himself with emotions befitting the occasion. But his thoughts teasingly gambolled about among the people

and things of the street. By-and-bye, however, he became sensible of his mental eye
being fixed upon the big fleshy mole on his
father's scantily bearded face. He recalled
the old man's carriage, the melancholy nod
of his head, his deep sigh upon taking snuff
from the time-honoured birch bark which
Jake had known as long as himself; and his
heart writhed with pity and with the acutest
pangs of homesickness. "And it was evening and it was morning, the sixth day. And
the heavens and the earth were finished."
As the Hebrew words of the Sanctification
of the Sabbath resounded in Jake's ears, in
his father's senile treble, he could see his
gaunt figure swaying over a pair of Sabbath
loaves. It is Friday night. The little room,
made tidy for the day of rest and faintly illuminated by the mysterious light of two
tallow candles rising from freshly burnished
candlesticks, is pervaded by a benign, re-
poseful warmth and a general air of peace
and solemnity. There, seated by the side of
the head of the little family and within easy

reach of the huge brick oven, is his old
mother, flushed with fatigue, and with an effort keeping her drowsy eyes open to attend,
with a devout mien, her husband's prayer.
Opposite to her, by the window, is Yekl, the
present Jake, awaiting his turn to chant the
same words in the holy tongue, and impatiently thinking of the repast to come after
it. Besides the three of them there is no
one else in the chamber, for Jake visioned
the fascinating scene as he had known it for
almost twenty years, and not as it had appeared during the short period since the
family had been joined by Gitl and subsequently by Yosselé.

Suddenly he felt himself a child, the only
and pampered son of a doting mother. He
was overcome with a heart-wringing consciousness of being an orphan, and his soul
was filled with a keen sense of desolation
and self-pity. And thereupon everything
around him—the rows of gigantic tenement
houses, the hum and buzz of the scurrying
pedestrians, the jingling horse cars—all sud-

denly grew alien and incomprehensible to
Jake. Ah, if he could return to his old
home and old days, and have his father recite
Sanctification again, and sit by his side, opposite to mother, and receive from her hand
a plate of reeking *tzimess,** as of yore!
Poor mother! He *will* not forget her—
But what is the Italian playing on that or-
gan, anyhow? Ah, it is the new waltz!
By the way, this is Monday and they are
dancing at Joe's now and he is not there.
" I shall not go there to-night, nor any other
night," he commiserated himself, his reveries
for the first time since he had left the Pitt
Street cigarette stand passing to his wife and
child. Her image now stood out in high
relief with the multitudinous noisy scene at
Joe's academy for a discordant, disquieting
background, amid which there vaguely de-
fined itself the reproachful saintlike visage
of the deceased. " I will begin a new life!"
he vowed to himself.

---

* A kind of dessert made of carrots or turnips.

He strove to remember the child's features, but could only muster the faintest rec-
ollection—scarcely anything beyond a general symbol—a red little thing smiling, as he,
Jake, tickles it under its tiny chin. Yet
Jake's finger at this moment seemed to feel
the soft touch of that little chin, and it sent
through him a thrill of fatherly affection to
which he had long been a stranger. Gitl, on
the other hand, loomed up in all the individual sweetness of her rustic face. He beheld
her kindly mouth opening wide—rather too
wide, but all the lovelier for it—as she
spoke; her prominent red gums, her little
black eyes. He could distinctly hear her
voice with her peculiar lisp, as one summer
morning she had burst into the house and,
clapping her hands in despair, she had cried,
"A weeping to me! The yellow rooster is
gone!" or, as coming into the smithy she
would say: "Father-in-law, mother-in-law
calls you to dinner. Hurry up, Yekl, dinner
is ready." And although this was all he could
recall her saying, Jake thought himself re-

tentive of every word she had ever uttered in his presence. His heart went out to Gitl and her environment, and he was seized with a yearning tenderness that made him feel like crying. ' " I would not exchange her little finger for all the American *ladas*," he soliloquized, comparing Gitl in his mind with the dancing-school girls of his circle. It now filled him with disgust to think of the morals of some of them, although it was from his own sinful experience that he knew them to be of a rather loose character.

He reached his lodgings in a devout mood, and before going to bed he was about to say his prayers. Not having said them for nearly three years, however, he found, to his dismay, that he could no longer do it by heart. His landlady had a prayer-book, but, unfortunately, she kept it locked in the bureau, and she was now asleep, as was everybody else in the house. Jake reluctantly undressed and went to bed on the kitchen lounge, where he usually slept.

When a boy his mother had taught him

to believe that to go to sleep at night without having recited the bed prayer rendered
one liable to be visited and choked in bed
by some ghost. Later, when he had grown
up, and yet before he had left his birthplace,
he had come to set down this earnest belief
of his good old mother as a piece of womanish superstition, while since he had settled
in America he had hardly ever had an occasion to so much as think of bed prayers.
Nevertheless, as he now lay vaguely listen-
ing to the weird ticking of the clock on the
mantelpiece over the stove, and at the same
time desultorily brooding upon his father's
death, the old belief suddenly uprose in his
mind and filled him with mortal terror. He
tried to persuade himself that it was a silly
notion worthy of womenfolk, and even affected to laugh at it audibly. But all in
vain. " Cho-king! Cho-king! Cho-king!"
went the clock, and the form of a man in
white burial clothes never ceased gleaming
in his face. He resolutely turned to the
wall, and, pulling the blanket over his head,

he huddled himself snugly up for instantaneous sleep. But presently he felt the cold
grip of a pair of hands about his throat, and
he even mentally stuck out his tongue, as
one does while being strangled.

With a fast-beating heart Jake finally
jumped off the lounge, and gently knocked
at the door of his landlady's bedroom.

"*Eshcoosh me, mishesh*, be so kind as to
lend me your prayer-book. I want to say
the night prayer," he addressed her imploringly.

The old woman took it for a cruel prac-
tical joke, and flew into a passion.

"Are you crazy or drunk? A nice time
to make fun!"

And it was not until he had said with
suppliant vehemence, "May I as surely be
alive as my father is dead!" and she had subjected him to a cross-examination, that she
expressed sympathy and went to produce
the keys.

CHAPTER IV.

THE MEETING.

A FEW weeks later, on a Saturday morning, Jake, with an unfolded telegram in his hand, stood in front of one of the desks at the Immigration Bureau of Ellis Island. He was freshly shaven and clipped, smartly dressed in his best clothes and ball shoes, and, in spite of the sickly expression of shamefacedness and anxiety which distorted his features, he looked younger than usual.

All the way to the island he had been in a flurry of joyous anticipation. The prospect of meeting his dear wife and child, and, incidentally, of showing off his swell attire to her, had thrown him into a fever of impatience. But on entering the big shed he had caught a distant glimpse of Gitl and Yosselé through the railing separating the detained immigrants from their visitors, and his heart had sunk at the sight of his wife's uncouth and (un-American) appearance. She was slovenly dressed in a brown jacket and skirt of grotesque cut, and her hair was concealed under a voluminous wig of a pitch-black hue. This she had put on just before leaving the steamer, both " in honour of the Sabbath " and by way of sprucing herself up for the great event. Since Yekl had left home she had gained considerably in the measurement of her waist. The wig, however, made her seem stouter and as though shorter than she would have appeared without it. It also added at least five years to her looks. But she was aware neither of this nor of the fact that in New York even a Jewess of her station and orthodox breeding is accustomed to blink at the wickedness of displaying her natural hair, and that none but an elderly matron may wear a wig with-

out being the occasional target for snow-
balls or stones. She was naturally dark of
complexion, and the nine or ten days spent
at sea had covered her face with a deep
bronze, which combined with her prominent
cheek bones, inky little eyes, and, above all,
the smooth black wig, to lend her resemblance to a squaw.

Jake had no sooner caught sight of her
than he had averted his face, as if loth to rest
his eyes on her, in the presence of the surg-
ing crowd around him, before it was inevita-
ble. He dared not even survey that crowd
to see whether it contained any acquaintance
of his, and he vaguely wished that her release
were delayed indefinitely.

Presently the officer behind the desk
took the telegram from him, and in another
little while Gitl, hugging Yosselé with one
arm and a bulging parcel with the other,
emerged from a side door.

"Yekl!" she screamed out in a piteous
high key, as if crying for mercy.

" Dot'sh alla right!" he returned in English, with a wan smile and unconscious of what he was saying. His wandering eyes and dazed mind were striving to fix themselves upon the stern functionary and the questions he bethought himself of asking before finally releasing his prisoners. The contrast between Gitl and Jake was so striking that the officer wanted to make sure—partly as a matter of official duty and partly for the fun of the thing—that the two were actually man and wife.

" *Oi* a lamentation upon me! He shaves his beard!" Gitl ejaculated to herself as she scrutinized her husband. " Yosselé, look! Here is *taté!* "

But Yosselé did not care to look at taté. Instead, he turned his frightened little eyes— precise copies of Jake's—and buried them in his mother's cheek.

When Gitl was finally discharged she made to fling herself on Jake. But he checked her by seizing both loads from her arms. He started for a distant and deserted corner of the room, bidding her follow. For

a moment the boy looked stunned, then he
burst out crying and fell to kicking his father's chest with might and main, his reddened little face appealingly turned to Gitl.
Jake continuing his way tried to kiss his son
into toleration, but the little fellow proved
too nimble for him.   It was in vain that
Gitl, scurrying behind, kept expostulating
with Yosselé : " Why, it is taté !"   Taté was
forced to capitulate before the march was
brought to its end.

At length, when the secluded corner had
been reached, and Jake and Gitl had set
down their burdens, husband and wife flew
into mutual embrace and fell to kissing each
other.   The performance had an effect of
something done to order, which, it must be
owned, was far from being belied by the
state of their minds at the moment.   Their
kisses imparted the taste of mutual estrange-
ment to both.   In Jake's case the sensation
was quickened by the strong steerage odours
which were emitted by Gitl's person, and he
involuntarily recoiled.

"You look like a *poritz*," * she said shyly.

" How are you ?   How is mother ? "

" How should she be ? So, so. She sends you her love," Gitl mumbled out.

" How long was father ill ? "

" Maybe a month.   He cost us health enough."

He proceeded to make advances to Yosselé, she appealing to the child in his behalf. For a moment the sight of her, as they were both crouching before the boy, precipitated a wave of thrilling memories on Jake and made him feel in his old environment. Presently, however, the illusion took wing and here he was, Jake the Yankee, with this bonnetless, wigged, dowdyish little greenhorn by his side ! That she was his wife, nay, that he was a married man at all, seemed incredible to him. The sturdy, thriving urchin had at first inspired him with pride ; but as he now cast another side glance at Gitl's wig he lost all interest in him, and began to regard

---

* Yiddish for nobleman.

6

him, together with his mother, as one great
obstacle dropped from heaven, as it were, in
his way.

Gitl, on her part, was overcome with a
feeling akin to awe. She, too, could not get
herself to realize that this stylish young man
—shaved and dressed as in Povodye is only
some young nobleman—was Yekl, her own
Yekl, who had all these three years never
been absent from her mind. And while she
was once more examining Jake's blue diagonal cutaway, glossy stand-up collar, the
white four-in-hand necktie, coquettishly
tucked away in the bosom of his starched
shirt, and, above all, his patent leather shoes,
she was at the same time mentally scanning
the Yekl of three years before. The latter
alone was hers, and she felt like crying to
the image to come back to her and let her
be *his* wife.

Presently, when they had got up and
Jake was plying her with perfunctory questions, she chanced to recognise a certain
movement of his upper lip—an old trick of

his. It was as if she had suddenly discovered her own Yekl in an apparent stranger, and, with another pitiful outcry, she fell on his breast.

" Don't ! " he said, with patient gentleness, pushing away her arms. " Here everything is so different."

She coloured deeply.

" They don't wear wigs here," he ventured to add.

" What then ? " she asked, perplexedly.

" You will see. It is quite another world."

" Shall I take it off, then ? I have a nice Saturday kerchief," she faltered. " It is of silk—I bought it at Kalmen's for a bargain. It is still brand new."

" Here one does not wear even a kerchief."

" How then ? Do they go about with their own hair ? " she queried in ill-disguised bewilderment.

" *Vell, alla right*, put it on, quick ! "

As she set about undoing her parcel, she

bade him face about and screen her, so that neither he nor any stranger could see her bareheaded while she was replacing the wig by the kerchief. He obeyed. All the while the operation lasted he stood with his gaze on the floor, gnashing his teeth with disgust and shame, or hissing some Bowery oath.

"Is this better?" she asked bashfully, when her hair and part of her forehead were hidden under a kerchief of flaming blue and yellow, whose end dangled down her back.

The kerchief had a rejuvenating effect. But Jake thought that it made her look like an Italian woman of Mulberry Street on Sunday.

"*Alla right*, leave it be for the present," he said in despair, reflecting that the wig would have been the lesser evil of the two.

When they reached the city Gitl was shocked to see him lead the way to a horse car.

"*Oi* woe is me! Why, it is Sabbath!" she gasped.

He irately essayed to explain that a car, being an uncommon sort of vehicle, riding in it implied no violation of the holy day. But this she sturdily met by reference to railroads. Besides, she had, seen horse cars while stopping in Hamburg, and knew that no orthodox Jew would use them on the seventh day. At length Jake, losing all self-control, fiercely commanded her not to make him the laughing-stock of the people on the street and to get in without further ado. As to the sin of the matter he was willing to take it all upon himself. Completely dismayed by his stern manner, amid the strange, uproarious, forbidding surroundings, Gitl yielded.

As the horses started she uttered a groan of consternation and remained looking aghast and with a violently throbbing heart. If she had been a culprit on the way to the gallows she could not have been more terrified than she was now at this her first ride on the day of rest.

The conductor came up for their fares.

Jake handed him a ten-cent piece, and raising two fingers, he roared out : " Two ! He
ain' no maur as tree years, de liddle feller ! "
And so great was the impression which his
dashing manner and his English produced
on Gitl, that for some time it relieved her
mind and she even forgot to be shocked by
the sight of her husband handling coin on
the Sabbath.

Having thus paraded himself before his
wife, Jake all at once grew kindly disposed
toward her.

" You must be hungry ? " he asked.

" Not at all ! Where do you eat your
varimess ? " *

" Don't say varimess," he corrected
her complaisantly ; " here it is called *dinner.*"

" *Dinner ?* † And what if one becomes
fatter ? " she confusedly ventured an irresisti-
ble pun.

---

* Yiddish for dinner.
† Yiddish for thinner.

This was the way in which Gitl came to receive her first lesson in the five or six score English words and phrases which the omnivorous Jewish jargon has absorbed in the Ghettos of English-speaking countries.

CHAPTER V.

It was early in the afternoon of Gitl's second Wednesday in the New World. Jake, Bernstein and Charley, their two boarders, were at work. Yosselé was sound asleep in the lodgers' double bed, in the smallest of the three tiny rooms which the family rented on the second floor of one of a row of brand-new tenement houses. Gitl was by herself in the little front room which served the quadruple purpose of kitchen, dining room, sitting room, and parlour. She wore a skirt and a loose jacket of white Russian calico, decorated with huge gay figures, and her dark hair was only half covered by a bandana of red and yellow. This was

Gitl's compromise between her conscience and her husband. She panted to yield to Jake's demands completely, but could not nerve herself up to going about "in her own hair, like a Gentile woman." Even the expostulations of Mrs. Kavarsky—the childless middle-aged woman who occupied with her husband the three rooms across the narrow hallway—failed to prevail upon her. Nevertheless Jake, succumbing to Mrs. Kavarsky's annoying solicitations, had bought his wife a cheap high-crowned hat, utterly unfit to be worn over her voluminous wig, and even a corset. Gitl could not be coaxed into accompanying them to the store; but the eloquent neighbour had persuaded Jake that her presence at the transaction was not indispensable after all.

"Leave it to me," she said; "I know what will become her and what won't. I'll get her a hat that will make a Fifth Avenue lady of her, and you shall see if she does not give in. If she is then not *satetzfiet* to go with her own hair, *vell!*" What then would take place Mrs. Kavarsky left unsaid.

The hat and the corset had been lying in the house now three days, and the neighbour's predictions had not yet come true, save for Gitl's prying once or twice into the pasteboard boxes in which those articles lay, otherwise unmolested, on the shelf over her bed.

The door was open. Gitl stood toying with the knob of the electric bell, and deriving much delight from the way the street door latch kept clicking under her magic touch two flights above. Finally she wearied of her diversion, and shutting the door she went to take a look at Yosselé. She found him fast asleep, and, as she was retracing her steps through her own and Jake's bedroom, her eye fell upon the paper boxes. She got up on the edge of her bed and, lifting the cover from the hatbox, she took a prolonged look at its contents. All at once her face brightened up with temptation. She went to fasten the hallway door of the

kitchen on its latch, and then regaining the
bedroom shut herself in. After a lapse of
some ten or fifteen minutes she re-emerged,
attired in her brown holiday dress in which
she had first confronted Jake on Ellis Island,
and with the tall black straw hat on her
head. Walking on tiptoe, as though about
to commit a crime, she crossed over to the
looking-glass. Then she paused, her eyes on
the door, to listen for possible footsteps.
Hearing none she faced the glass. "Quite
a *panenke*!"* she thought to herself, all
aglow with excitement, a smile, at once
shamefaced and beatific, melting her features.
She turned to the right, then to the left, to
view herself in profile, as she had seen Mrs.
Kavarsky do, and drew back a step to ascertain the effect of the corset. To tell the
truth, the corset proved utterly impotent
against the baggy shapelessness of the Povodye garment. Yet Gitl found it to work
wonders, and readily pardoned it for the very

---

* A young noblewoman.

uncomfortable sensation which it caused her. She viewed herself again and again, and was in a flutter both of ecstasy and alarm when there came a timid rap on the door. Trembling all over, she scampered on tiptoe back into the bedroom, and after a little she returned in her calico dress and bandana kerchief. The knock at the door had apparently been produced by some peddler or beggar, for it was not repeated. Yet so violent was Gitl's agitation that she had to sit down on the haircloth lounge for breath and to regain composure.

"What is it they call this?" she presently asked herself, gazing at the bare boards of the floor. "Floor!" she recalled, much to her self-satisfaction. "And that?" she further examined herself, as she fixed her glance on the ceiling. This time the answer was slow in coming, and her heart grew faint. "And what was it Yekl called that?"—transferring her eyes to the window. "Veen—neev—veenda," she at last uttered exultantly. The evening before she had happened to call it *fentzter*, in spite of Jake's repeated corrections.

"Can't you say *veenda?*" he had growled. "What a peasant head! Other greenhornsh learn to speak American *shtyle* very fast; and she—one might tell her the same word eighty thousand times, and it is *nu used.*"

"*Es is of'n veenda mein ich,*"* she hastened to set herself right.

She blushed as she said it, but at the moment she attached no importance to the matter and took no more notice of it. Now, however, Jake's tone of voice, as he had rebuked her backwardness in picking up American Yiddish, came back to her and she grew dejected.

She was getting used to her husband, in whom her own Yekl and Jake the stranger were by degrees merging themselves into one undivided being. When the hour of his coming from work drew near she would

---

* It is on the window, I meant to say.

every little while consult the clock and become impatient with the slow progress of its
hands; although mixed with this impatience
there was a feeling of apprehension lest the
supper, prepared as it was under culinary
conditions entirely new to her, should fail to
please Jake and the boarders. She had even
become accustomed to address her husband
as Jake without reddening in the face; and,
what is more, was getting to tolerate herself
being called by him Goitie (Gertie)—a word
phonetically akin to Yiddish for Gentile.
For the rest she was too inexperienced and
too simple-hearted naturally to comment
upon his manner toward her. She had not
altogether overcome her awe of him, but as
he showed her occasional marks of kindness
she was upon the whole rather content with
her new situation. Now, however, as she
thus sat in solitude, with his harsh voice ringing in her ears and his icy look before her, a
feeling of suspicion darkened her soul. She
recalled other scenes where he had looked
and spoken as he had done the night before.

"He must hate me! A pain upon me!" she concluded with a fallen heart. She wondered whether his demeanour toward her was like that of other people who hated their wives. She remembered a woman of her native village who was known to be thus afflicted, and she dropped her head in a fit of despair. At one moment she took a firm resolve to pluck up courage and cast away the kerchief and the wig ; but at the next she reflected that God would be sure to punish her for the terrible sin, so that instead of winning Jake's love the change would increase his hatred for her. It flashed upon her mind to call upon some "good Jew" to pray for the return of his favour, or to seek some old Polish beggar woman who could prescribe a love potion. But then, alas! who knows whether there are in this terrible America any good Jews or beggar women with love potions at all! Better she had never known this "black year" of a country! Here everybody says she is green. What an ugly word to apply to people!

She had never been green at home, and here
she had suddenly become so. What do they
mean by it, anyhow? Verily, one might
turn green and yellow and gray while young
in such a dreadful place. Her heart was
wrung with the most excruciating pangs of
homesickness. And as she thus sat brooding and listlessly surveying her new surroundings—the iron stove, the stationary
washtubs, the window opening vertically,
the fire escape, the yellowish broom with its
painted handle—things which she had never
dreamed of at her birthplace—these objects
seemed to stare at her haughtily and inspired
her with fright. Even the burnished cup of
the electric bell knob looked contemptuous-
ly and seemed to call her "Greenhorn!
greenhorn!" "Lord of the world! Where
am I?" she whispered with tears in her
voice.

The dreary solitude terrified her, and she
instinctively rose to take refuge at Yosselé's
bedside. As she got up, a vague doubt came
over her whether she should find there her

child at all. But Yosselé was found safe
and sound enough. He was rubbing his
eyes and announcing the advent of his fa-
mous appetite. She seized him in her arms
and covered his warm cheeks with fervent
kisses which did her aching heart good.
And by-and-bye, as she admiringly watched
the boy making savage inroads into a generous slice of rye bread, she thought of Jake's
affection for the child; whereupon things began to assume a brighter aspect, and she
presently set about preparing supper with a
lighter heart, although her countenance for
some time retained its mournful woe-be-
gone expression.

Meanwhile Jake sat at his machine merrily pushing away at a cloak and singing to
it some of the popular American songs of
the day.

The sensation caused by the arrival of
his wife and child had nearly blown over.
Peltner's dancing school he had not visited
since a week or two previous to Gitl's land-

7

ing. As to the scene which had greeted him in the shop after the stirring news had first reached it, he had faced it out with much more courage and got over it with much less difficulty than he had anticipated.

"Did I ever tell you I was a *tzingle man?*" he laughingly defended himself, though blushing crimson, against his shopmates' taunts. "And am I obliged to give you a *report* whether my wife has come or not? You are not worth mentioning her name to, *anyhoy.*"

The boss then suggested that Jake celebrate the event with two pints of beer, the motion being seconded by the presser, who volunteered to fetch the beverage. Jake obeyed with alacrity, and if there had still lingered any trace of awkwardness in his position it was soon washed away by the foaming liquid.

As a matter of fact, Fanny's embarrassment was much greater than Jake's. The stupefying news was broken to her on the very day of Gitl's arrival. After passing a sleepless night she felt that she could not bring herself to face Jake in the presence of her other shopmates, to whom her feelings for him were an open secret. As luck would have it, it was Sunday, the beginning of a new working week in the metropolitan Ghetto, and she went to look for a job in another place.

Jake at once congratulated himself upon her absence and missed her. But then he equally missed the company of Mamie and of all the other dancing-school girls, whose society and attentions now more than ever seemed to him necessities of his life. They haunted his mind day and night; he almost never beheld them in his imagination except as clustering together with his fellow-cavaliers and making merry over him and his wife; and the vision pierced his heart with shame and jealousy. All his achievements seemed wiped out by a sudden stroke of ill fate. He thought himself a martyr, an innocent exile from a world to which he belonged by right; and he frequently felt the

sobs of self-pity mounting to his throat.
For several minutes at a time, while kicking
at his treadle, he would see, reddening before
him, Gitl's bandana kerchief and her prominent gums, or hear an un-American piece of
Yiddish pronounced with Gitl's peculiar lisp
—that very lisp, which three years ago he
used to mimic fondly, but which now grated
on his nerves and was apt to make his face
twitch with sheer disgust, insomuch that he
often found a vicious relief in mocking that
lisp of hers audibly over his work. But can
it be that he is doomed for life? No! no!
he would revolt, conscious at the same time
that there was really no escape. "Ah, may
she be killed, the horrid greenhorn!" he
would gasp to himself in a paroxysm of despair. And then he would bewail his lost
youth, and curse all Russia for his premature
marriage. Presently, however, he would recall the plump, spunky face of his son who
bore such close resemblance to himself, to
whom he was growing more strongly attached every day, and who was getting to

prefer his company to his mother's; and thereupon his heart would soften toward Gitl, and he would gradually feel the qualms of pity and remorse, and make a vow to treat her kindly. " Never min'," he would at such instances say in his heart, " she will *oyshgreen* * herself and I shall get used to her. She is a —— *shight* better than all the dancing-school girls." And he would inspire himself with respect for her spotless purity, and take comfort in the fact of her being a model housewife, undiverted from her duties by any thoughts of balls or picnics. And despite a deeper consciousness which exposed his readiness to sacrifice it all at any time, he would work himself into a dignified feeling as the head of a household and the father of a promising son, and soothe himself with the additional consolation that sooner or later the other fellows of Joe's academy would also be married.

---

* A verb coined from the Yiddish *oys*, out, and the English *green*, and signifying to cease being green.

On the Wednesday in question Jake and
his shopmates had warded off a reduction of
wages by threatening a strike, and were accordingly in high feather. And so Jake and
Bernstein came home in unusually good
spirits. Little Joey—for such was Yosselé's
name now—with whom his father's plays
were for the most part of an athletic character, welcomed Jake by a challenge for a pu-
gilistic encounter, and the way he said
"Coom a fight!" and held out his little fists
so delighted Mr. Podkovnik, Sr., that upon
ordering Gitl to serve supper he vouchsafed
a fillip on the tip of her nose.

While she was hurriedly setting the table,
Jake took to describing to Charley his em-
ployer's defeat. "You should have seen how
he looked, the cockroach!" he said. "He
became as pale as the wall and his teeth
were chattering as if he had been shaken
up with fever, *'pon my void.* And how
quiet he became all of a sudden, as if he
could not count two! One might apply him
to an ulcer, so soft was he—ha-ha-ha!" he

laughed, looking to Bernstein, who smiled assent.

At last supper was announced. Bernstein donned his hat, and did not sit down to the repast before he had performed his ablutions and whispered a short prayer. As he did so Jake and Charley interchanged a wink. As to themselves, they dispensed with all devotional preliminaries, and took their seats with uncovered heads. Gitl also washed her fingers and said the prayer, and as she handed Yosselé his first slice of bread she did not release it before he had recited the benediction.

Bernstein, who, as a rule, looked daggers at his meal, this time received his plate of *borshtch* *—his favourite dish—with a radiant face ; and as he ate he pronounced it a masterpiece, and lavished compliments on the artist.

" It's a long time since I tasted such a borshtch ! Simply a vivifier ! It melts in

---

* A sour soup of cabbage and beets.

every limb!" he kept rhapsodizing, between
mouthfuls. "It ought to be sent to the Chicago Exposition. ' The *missess* would get a
medal."

"A *regely* European borshtch!" Charley
chimed in. "It is worth ten cents a spoonful, *'pon mine vort!*"

"Go away! You are only making fun
of me," Gitl declared, beaming with pride.
"What is there to be laughing at? I
make it as well as I can," she added de-
murely.

"Let him who is laughing laugh with
teeth," jested Charlie. "I tell you it is a
——" The remainder of the sentence was
submerged in a mouthful of the vivifying
semi-liquid.

"*Alla right!*" Jake bethought himself.
"*Charge* him ten *shent* for each spoonful.
Mr. Bernstein, you shall be kind enough to
be the *bookkeeper*. But if you don't pay,
Chollie, I'll get out a *tzommesh* [summons]
from *court*."

Whereat the little kitchen rang with

laughter, in which all participated except Bernstein. Even Joey, or Yosselé, joined in the general outburst of merriment. Otherwise he was busily engaged cramming borshtch into his mouth, and, in passing, also into his nose, with both his plump hands for a pair of spoons. From time to time he would interrupt operations to make a wry face and, blinking his eyes, to lisp out rapturously, " Sour ! "

" Look—may you live long—do look ; he is laughing, too ! " Gitl called attention to Yosselé's bespattered face. " To think of such a crumb having as much sense as that ! " She was positive that he appreciated his father's witticism, although she herself understood it but vaguely.

" May he know evil no better than he knows what he is laughing at," Jake objected, with a fatherly mien. " What makes you laugh, Joey ? " The boy had no time to spare for an answer, being too busy licking his emptied plate. " Look at the soldier's appetite he has, *de feller !* Joey, hoy you like de borshtch? Alla right?" Jake asked in English.

"Awrr-ra rr-right!" Joey pealed out his sturdy rustic r's, which he had mastered shortly before taking leave of his doting grandmother.

"See how well he speaks English?" Jake said, facetiously. "A —— *shight* better than his mamma, *anyvay.*"

Gitl, who was in the meantime serving the meat, coloured, but took the remark in good part.

"*I tell ye* he is growing to be Presdent 'Nited States," Charlie interposed.

"*Greenhorn* that you are! A President must be American born," Jake explained, self-consciously. "Ain't it, Mr. Bernstein?"

"It's a pity, then, that he was not born in this country," Bernstein replied, his eye envyingly fixed now on Gitl, now at the child, on whose plate she was at this moment carving a piece of meat into tiny morsels. "*Vell*, if he cannot be a President of the United States, he may be one of a synagogue, so he is a president."

"Don't you worry for his sake," Gitl put in, delighted with the attention her son was absorbing. "He does not need to be a pesdent; he is growing to be a rabbi; don't be making fun of him." And she turned her head to kiss the future rabbi.

"Who is making fun?" Bernstein demurred. "I wish I had a boy like him."

"Get married and you will have one," said Gitl, beamingly.

"*Shay*, Mr. Bernstein, how about your *shadchen*?"* Jake queried. He gave a laugh, but forthwith checked it, remaining with an embarrassed grin on his face, as though anxious to swallow the question. Bernstein blushed to the roots of his hair, and bent an irate glance on his plate, but held his peace.

His reserved manner, if not his superior education, held Bernstein's shopmates at a

---

* A matrimonial agent.

respectful distance from him, and, as a rule,
rendered him proof against their badinage,
although behind his back they would in-
dulge, an occasional joke on his inferiority
as a workman, and—while they were at it
—on his dyspepsia, his books, and staid,
methodical habits. Recently, however, they
had got wind of his clandestine visits to a
marriage broker's, and the temptation to
chaff him on the subject had proved resist-
less, all the more so because Bernstein,
whose leading foible was his well-controlled
vanity, was quick to take offence in general,
and on this matter in particular. As to Jake,
he was by no means averse to having a
laugh at somebody else's expense ; but since
Bernstein had become his boarder he felt
that he could not afford to wound his pride.
Hence his regret and anxiety at his allusion
to the matrimonial agent.

. After supper Charlie went out for the
evening, while Bernstein retired to their little bedroom. Gitl busied herself with the
dishes, and Jake took to romping about with

Joey and had a hearty laugh with him. He was beginning to tire of the boy's company and to feel lonesome generally, when there was a knock at the door. ·

"Coom in!" Gitl hastened to say somewhat coquettishly, flourishing her proficiency in American manners, as she raised her head from the pot in her hands.

"Coom in!" repeated Joey.

The door flew open, and in came Mamie, preceded by a cloud of cologne odours. She was apparently dressed for some occasion of state, for she was powdered and straight-laced and resplendent in a waist of blazing red, gaudily trimmed, and with puff sleeves, each wider than the vast expanse of white straw, surmounted with a whole forest of ostrich feathers, which adorned her head. One of her gloved hands held the huge hoop-shaped yellowish handle of a blue parasol.

"Good-evenin', Jake!" she said, with ostentatious vivacity.

"Good-evenin', Mamie!" Jake returned,

jumping to his feet and violently reddening,
as if suddenly pricked. "Mish Fein, my
vife! My vife, Mish Fein!"

Miss Fein made a stately bow, primly
biting her lip as she did so. Gitl, with the
pot in her hands, stood staring sheepishly, at
a loss what to do.

"Say 'I'm glyad to meech you,'" Jake
urged her, confusedly.

The English phrase was more than Gitl
could venture to echo.

"She is still *green*," Jake apologized for
her, in Yiddish.

"*Never min*', she will soon *oysgreen* herself," Mamie remarked, with patronizing affa-
bility.

"The *lada* is an acquaintance of mine,"
Jake explained bashfully, his hand feeling the few days' growth of beard on his
chin.

Gitl instinctively scented an enemy in
the visitor, and eyed her with an uneasy gaze.
Nevertheless she mustered a hospitable air,
and drawing up the rocking chair, she said,

with shamefaced cordiality: "Sit down; why
should you be standing? You may be seated for the same money."

In the conversation which followed Mamie did most of the talking. With a nervous volubility often broken by an irrelevant
giggle, and violently rocking with her chair,
she expatiated on the charms of America,
prophesying that her hostess would bless the
day of her arrival on its soil, and went off in
ecstasies over Joey. She spoke with an
overdone American accent in the dialect of
the Polish Jews, affectedly Germanized and
profusely interspersed with English, so that
Gitl, whose mother tongue was Lithuanian
Yiddish, could scarcely catch the meaning of
one half of her flood of garrulity. And as
she thus rattled on, she now examined the
room, now surveyed Gitl from head to foot,
now fixed her with a look of studied sarcasm, followed by a side glance at Jake,
which seemed to say, "Woe to you, what a
rag of a wife yours is!" Whenever Gitl
ventured a timid remark, Mamie would nod

assent with dignified amiability, and thereupon imitate a smile, broad yet fleeting,
which she had seen performed by some up-
town ladies.

Jake stared at the lamp with a faint
simper, scarcely following the caller's words.
His head swam with embarrassment. The
consciousness of Gitl's unattractive appearance made him sick with shame and vexa-
tion, and his eyes carefully avoided her bandana, as a culprit schoolboy does the evidence
of his offence.

" You mush vant you tventy-fife dollars,"
he presently nerved himself up to say in
English, breaking an awkward pause.

" I should cough ! " Mamie rejoined.

" In a coupel a veeksh, Mamie, as sure as
my name is Jake."

" In a couple o' veeks ! No, sirree ! I
mus' have my money at oncet. I don' know
vere you vill get it, dough. Vy, a married
man ! "—with a chuckle. " You got a —— of
a lot o' t'ings to pay for. You took de foi-
nitsha by a custom peddler, ain' it ? But

what a —— do *I* care? I vant my money.
I voiked hard enough for it."

"Don' shpeak English. She'll t'ink I
don' knu vot ve shpeakin'," he besought her,
in accents which implied intimacy between
the two of them and a common aloofness
from Gitl.

"Vot d'I care vot she t'inks? She's your
vife, ain' it? Vell, she mus' know ev'ry-
t'ing. Dot's right! A husban' dass'n't hide
not'ink from his vife!"—with another chuckle
and another look of deadly sarcasm at Gitl.
"I can say de same in Jewish——"

"Shurr-r up, Mamie!" he interrupted her,
gaspingly.

"Don'tch you like it, lump it! A vife
mus'n't be skinned like a strange lady, see?"
she pursued inexorably. "O'ly a strange
goil a feller might bluff dot he ain' married,
and skin her out of tventy-five dollars." In
point of fact, he had never directly given
himself out for a single man to her. But it
did not even occur to him to defend himself
on that score.

8

"Mamie! Ma-a-mie! Shtop! I'll pay
you ev'ry shent. Shpeak Jewesh, pleashe!"
he implored, as if for life.

"You'r' afraid of her? Dot's right!
Dot's right! Dot's nice! All religious peoples is afraid of deir vifes. But vy didn' you
say you vas married from de sta't, an' dot
you vant money to send for dem?" she tor-
tured him, with a lingering arch leer.

"For Chrish' shake, Mamie!" he entreat-
ed her, wincingly. "Shtop to shpeak English, an' shpeak shomet'ing differench. I'll
shee you—vere can I shee you?"

"You von't come by Joe no more?" she
asked, with sudden interest and even solici-
tude.

"You t'ink indeed I'm 'frait? If I vanted I can gu dere more ash I ushed to gu
dere. But vere can I findsh you?"

"I guess you know vere I'm livin', don'ch
you? So kvick you forget? Vot a sho't
mind you got! Vill you come? Never
min', I know you are only bluffin', an' dot's
all."

" I'll come, ash sure ash I leev."

"Vill you? All right. But if you don'
come an' pay me at least ten dollars for a
sta't, you'll see!"

In the meanwhile Gitl, poor thing, sat
pale and horror-struck. Mamie's perfumes
somehow terrified her. She was racked with
jealousy and all sorts of suspicions, which she
vainly struggled to disguise. She could see
that they were having a heated altercation,
and that Jake was begging about something
or other, and was generally the under dog in
the parley. Ever and anon she strained her
ears in the effort to fasten some of the incomprehensible sounds in her memory, that
she might subsequently parrot them over to
Mrs. Kavarsky, and ascertain their meaning.
But, alas! the attempt proved futile; "never
min'" and "all right" being all she could
catch.

Mamie concluded her visit by presenting
Joey with the imposing sum of five cents.

"What do you say? Say 'danks, sir!'"
Gitl prompted the boy.

"Shay 't'ank you, ma'am!'" Jake overruled her. "'Shir' is said to a gentlemarn."

"Good-night!" Mamie sang out, as she
majestically opened the door.

"Good-night!" Jake returned, with a
burning face.

"Goot-night!" Gitl and Joey chimed in
duet.

"Say 'cull again!'"

"Cullye gain!"

"Good-night!" Mamie said once more,
as she bowed herself out of the door with
what she considered an exquisitely "tony"
smile.

The guest's exit was succeeded by a momentary silence. Jake felt as if his face and
ears were on fire.

"We used to work in the same shop," he
presently said.

"Is that the way a seamstress dresses in
America?" Gitl inquired. "It is not for
nothing that it is called the golden land,"
she added, with timid irony.

"She must be going to a ball," he explained, at the same moment casting a glance at the looking-glass.

The word "ball" had an imposing ring for Gitl's ears. At home she had heard it used in connection with the sumptuous life of the Russian or Polish nobility, but had never formed a clear idea of its meaning.

"She looks a veritable *panenke*,"* she remarked, with hidden sarcasm. "Was she born here?"

"*Nu*, but she has been very long here. She speaks English like one American born. We are used to speak in English when we talk *shop*. She came to ask me about a *job*."

Gitl reflected that with Bernstein Jake was in the habit of talking shop in Yiddish, although the boarder could even read English books, which her husband could not do.

---

* A young noblewoman.

CHAPTER VI.

CIRCUMSTANCES ALTER CASES.

JAKE was left by Mamie in a state of unspeakable misery. He felt discomfited, crushed, the universal butt of ridicule. Her perfumes lingered in his nostrils, taking his breath away. Her venomous gaze stung his heart. She seemed to him elevated above the social plane upon which he had recently (though the interval appeared very long) stood by her side, nay, upon which he had had her at his beck and call; while he was degraded, as it were, wallowing in a mire, from which he yearningly looked up to his former equals, vainly begging for recognition. An uncontrollable desire took possession of him to run after her, to have an explanation, and to swear that he was the same Jake and as much of a Yankee and a gallant as ever. But here was his wife fixing him with a timid, piteous look, which at once exasperated and cowed him ; and he dared not stir out of the house, as though nailed by that look of hers to the spot.

He lay down on the lounge, and shut his eyes. Gitl dutifully brought him a pillow. As she adjusted it under his head the touch of her hand on his face made him shrink, as if at the contact with a reptile. He was anxious to flee from his wretched self into oblivion, and his wish was soon gratified, the combined effect of a hard day's work and a plentiful and well-relished supper plunging him into a heavy sleep.

While his snores resounded in the little kitchen, Gitl put the child to bed, and then passed with noiseless step into the boarders' room. The door was ajar and she entered it without knocking, as was her wont. She found Bernstein bent over a book, with a ponderous dictionary by its side. A kero-

sene lamp with a red shade, occupying nearly all the remaining space on the table,
spread a lurid mysterious light. Gitl asked
the studious cloakmaker whether he knew a
Polish girl named Mamie Fein.

"Mamie Fein? No. Why?" said Bernstein, with his index finger on the passage
he had been reading, and his eyes on Gitl's
plumpish cheek, bathed in the roseate light.

"Nothing. May not one ask?"

"What is the matter? Speak out! Are
you afraid to tell me?" he insisted.

"What should be the matter? She was
here. A nice *lada*."

"Your husband knows many nice *ladies*,"
he said, with a faint but significant smile.
And immediately regretting the remark he
went on to smooth it down by characterizing Jake as an honest and good-natured fellow.

"You ought to think yourself fortu-
nate in having him for your husband," he
added.

"Yes, but what did you mean by what

you said first?" she demanded, with an anxious air.

"What did I mean? What should I have meant? I meant what I said. '*F cou'se* he knows many girls. But who does not? You know there are always girls in the shops where we work. Never fear, Jake has nothing to do with them."

"Who says I fear! Did I say I did? Why should I?"

Encouraged by the cheering effect which his words were obviously having on the credulous, unsophisticated woman, he pursued: "May no Jewish daughter have a worse husband. Be easy, be easy. I tell you he is melting away for you. He never looked as happy as he does since you came."

"Go away! You must be making fun of me!" she said, beaming with delight.

"Don't you believe me? Why, are you not a pretty young woman?" he remarked, with an oily look in his eye.

The crimson came into her cheek, and she lowered her glance.

"Stop making fun of me, I beg you," she said softly. " Is it true?"

" Is what true? That you are a pretty young woman? Take a looking-glass and see for yourself."

"Strange man that you are!" she returned, with confused deprecation. " I mean what you said before about Jake," she faltered.

"Oh, about Jake! Then say so," he jested. " Really he loves you as life."

" How do you know?" she queried, wistfully.

" How do I know!" he repeated, with an amused smile. "As if one could not see!"

" But he never told you himself!"

" How do you know he did not? You have guessed wrongly, see! He did, lots of times," he concluded gravely, touched by the anxiety of the poor woman.

.She left Bernstein's room all thrilling with• joy, and repentant for her excess of communicativeness. "A wife must not tell other people what happens to her husband,"

she lectured herself, in the best of humours.
Still, the words "Your husband knows many
nice *ladas*," kept echoing at the bottom of
her soul, and in another few minutes she was
at Mrs. Kavarsky's, confidentially describing
Mamie's visit as well as her talk with the
boarder, omitting nothing save the latter's
compliments to her looks.

Mrs. Kavarsky was an eccentric, scraggy
little woman, with a vehement manner and
no end of words and gesticulations. Her
dry face was full of warts and surmounted by
a chaotic mass of ringlets and curls of a
faded brown. None too tidy about her person, and rather slattern in general appearance, she zealously kept up the over-scrupu-
lous cleanliness for which the fame of her
apartments reached far and wide. Her
neighbours and townsfolk pronounced her
crazy but "with a heart of diamond," that is
to say, the diametrical opposite of the pre-
cious stone in point of hardness, and resem-
bling it in the general sense of excellence of
quality. She was neighbourly enough, and

as she was the most prosperous and her establishment the best equipped in the whole
tenement, many a woman would come to
borrow some cooking utensil or other, or
even a few dollars on rent day, which Mrs.
Kavarsky always started by refusing in the
most pointed terms, and almost always finished by granting.

She started to listen to Gitl's report with
a fierce mien which gradually thawed into a
sage smile. When the young neighbour
had rested her case, she first nodded her
head, as who should say, " What fools this
young generation be!" and then burst out:

" Do you know what *I* have to tell you?
Guess!"

Gitl thought Heaven knows what revela-
tions awaited her.

"That you are a lump of horse and a
greenhorn and nothing else!" (Gitl felt
much relieved.) "That piece of ugliness
should *try* and come to *my* house! Then
she would know the price of a pound of evil.
I should open the door and—*march* to

eighty black years! Let her go to where she came from! America is not Russia, thanked be the Lord of the world. Here one must only know how to handle a husband. Here a husband must remember '*ladas foist*'—but then you do not even know what that means!" she exclaimed, with a despairing wave of her hand.

"What does it mean?" Gitl inquired, pensively.

"What does it mean? What should it mean? It means but too well, *never min'*. It means that when a husband does not *behabe* as he should, one does not stroke his cheeks for it. A prohibition upon me if one does. If the wife is no greenhorn she gets him shoved into the oven, over there, across the river."

"You mean they send him to prison?"

"Where else—to the theatre?" Mrs. Kavarsky mocked her furiously.

"A weeping to me!" Gitl said, with horror. "May God save me from such things!"

In due course Mrs. Kavarsky arrived at

the subject of head-gear, and for the third or
fourth time she elicited from her pupil a
promise to discard the kerchief and to sell
the wig.

"No wonder he does hate you, seeing
you in that horrid rag, which makes a grandma of you. Drop it, I tell you! Drop it so
that no survivor nor any refugee is left of it.
If you don't obey me this time, dare not
cross my threshold any more, do you hear?"
she thundered. "One might as well talk to
the wall as to her!" she proceeded, actually
addressing herself to the opposite wall of her
kitchen, and referring to her interlocutrice in
the third person. "I am working and working for her, and here she appreciates it as
much as the cat. Fie!" With which the
irate lady averted her face in disgust.

"I shall take it off; now for sure—as
sure as this is Wednesday," said Gitl, beseech-
ingly.

Mrs. Kavarsky turned back to her paci-
fied.

"Remember now! If you *deshepoitn*

[disappoint] me this time, well!—look at me! I should think I was no Gentile woman, either. I am as pious as you *anyhull*, and come from no mean family, either. You know I hate to boast; *but* my father—peace be upon him!—was fit to be a rabbi. *Vell*, and yet I am not afraid to go with my own hair. May no greater sins be committed! Then it would be *never min'* enough. Plenty of time for putting on the patch [meaning the wig] when I get old; *but* as long as I am young, I am young *an' dot's ull!* It can not be helped; when one lives in an *edzecate* country, one must live like *edzecate peoples*. As they play, so one dances, as the saying is. But I think it is time for you to be going. Go, my little kitten," Mrs. Kavarsky said, suddenly lapsing into accents of the most tender affection. " He may be up by this time and wanting *tea*. Go, my little lamb, go and *try* to make yourself agreeable to him and the Uppermost will help. In America one must take care not to displease a husband. Here one is to-day in New

York and to-morrow in Chicago; do you
understand? As if there were any shame or
decency here! A father is no father, a wife,
no wife—*not'ing!* Go now, my baby! Go
and throw away your rag and be a nice woman, and everything will be *ull right.*"
And so hurrying Gitl to go, she detained her
with ever a fresh torrent of loquacity for another ten minutes, till the young woman,
standing on pins and needles and scarcely
lending an ear, plucked up courage to plead
her household duties and take a hasty de-
parture.

She found Jake fast asleep. It was after
eleven when he slowly awoke. He got up
with a heavy burden on his soul—a vague
sense of having met with some horrible re-
buff. In his semiconsciousness he was una-
ware, however, of his wife's and son's existence and of the change which their advent
had produced in his life, feeling himself the
same free bird that he had been a fortnight
ago. He stared about the room, as if wondering where he was. Noticing Gitl, who at

that moment came out of the bedroom, he instantly realized the situation, recalling Mamie, hat, perfumes, and all, and his heart sank within him. The atmosphere of the room became stifling to him. After sitting on the lounge for some time with a drooping head, he was tempted to fling himself on the pillow again, but instead of doing so he slipped on his hat and coat and went out.

Gitl was used to his goings and comings without explanation. Yet this time his slam of the door sent a sharp pang through her heart. She had no doubt but that he was bending his steps to another interview with the Polish witch, as she mentally branded Miss Fein.

Nor was she mistaken, for Jake did start, mechanically, in the direction of Chrystie Street, where Mamie lodged. He felt sure that she was away to some ball, but the very house in which she roomed seemed to draw him with magnetic force. Moreover, he had a lurking hope that he might, after all, find her about the building. Ah, if by a

9

stroke of good luck he came upon her on the street! All he wished was to have a talk, and that for the sole purpose of amending her unfavourable impression of him. Then he would never so much as think of Mamie, for, indeed, she was hateful to him, he persuaded himself.

Arrived at his destination, and failing to find Mamie on the sidewalk, he was tempted to wait till she came from the ball, when he was seized with a sudden sense of the impropriety of his expedition, and he forthwith returned home, deciding in his mind, as he walked, to move with his wife and child to Chicago.

Meanwhile Mamie lay brooding in her cot-bed in the parlour, which she shared with her landlady's two daughters. She was in the most wretched frame of mind, ineffectually struggling to fall asleep. She had made her way down the stairs leading from the Podkovniks with a violently palpitating heart. She had been bound for no more imposing a place than Joe's academy, and

before repairing thither she had had to betake herself home to change her stately toilet for a humbler attire.   For, as a matter of
fact, it was expressly for her visit to the Podkovniks that she had thus pranked herself
out, and that would have been much too
gorgeous an appearance to make at Joe's
establishment on one of its regular dancing
evenings.   Having changed her toilet she
did call at Joe's; but so full was her mind
of Jake and his wife and, accordingly, she
was so irritable, that in the middle of a qua-
drille she picked a quarrel with the dancing
master, and abruptly left the hall.

The next day Jake's work fared badly.
When it was at last over he did not go direct home as usual, but first repaired to Mamie's.   He found her with her landlady in
the kitchen.   She looked careworn and was
in a white blouse which lent her face a con-
valescent, touching effect.

"Good-eveni'g, Mrs. Bunetzky! Good-
eveni'g, Mamie!" he fairly roared, as he play-

fully fillipped his hat backward. And after addressing a pleasantry or two to the mistress of the house, he boldly proposed to her boarder to go out with him for a talk. For a moment Mamie hesitated, fearing lest her landlady had become aware of the existence of a Mrs. Podkovnik ; but instantly flinging all considerations to the wind, she followed him out into the street.

"You'sh afraid I vouldn't pay you, Mamie?" he began, with bravado, in spite of his intention to start on a different line, he knew not exactly which.

Mamie was no less disappointed by the opening of the conversation than he. "I ain't afraid a bit," she answered, sullenly.

"Do you think my *kshpenshesh* are larger now?" he resumed in Yiddish. "May I lose as much through sickness. On the contrary, I *shpend* even much less than I used to. We have two nice boarders—I keep them only for company's sake—and I have a *shteada job—a puddin' of a job*. I shall

have still more money to *shpend outshite*,"
he added, falteringly.

"Outside?"—and she burst into an arti-
ficial laugh which sent the blood to Jake's face.

"Why, do you think I sha'n't go to Joe's,
nor to the theatre, nor anywhere any more?
Still oftener than before! *Hoy much vill
you bet?*"

"*Rats!* A married man, a papa go to a
dancing school! Not unless your wife drags
along with you and never lets go of your
skirts," she said sneeringly, adding the decla-
ration that Jake's "bluffs" gave her a "reg-
ula' pain in de neck."

Jake, writhing under her lashes, protested
his freedom as emphatically as he could; but
it only served to whet Mamie's spite, and
against her will she went on twitting him as
a henpecked husband and an old-fashioned
Jew. Finally she reverted to the subject of
his debt, whereupon he took fire, and after
an interchange of threats and some quite
forcible language they parted company.

.   .   .   .   .   .

From that evening the spectre of Mamie
dressed in her white blouse almost unremit-
tingly preyed on Jake's mind. The mournful sneer which had lit her pale, invalid-look-
ing face on their last interview, when she
wore that blouse, relentlessly stared down
into his heart; gnawed at it with tantalizing
deliberation ; " drew out his soul," as he once
put it to himself, dropping his arms and head
in despair. " Is this what they call love?"
he wondered, thinking of the strange, hither-
to unexperienced kind of malady, which
seemed to be gradually consuming his whole
being. He felt as if Mamie had breathed a
delicious poison into his veins, which was
now taking effect, spreading a devouring
fire through his soul, and kindling him with
a frantic thirst for more of the same virus.
His features became distended, as it were,
and acquired a feverish effect; his eyes had a
pitiable, beseeching look, like those of a
child in the period of teething.

He grew more irritable with Gitl every
day, the energy failing him to dissemble his

hatred for her. There were moments when, in his hopeless craving for the presence of Mamie, he would consciously seek refuge in a feeling of compunction and of pity for his wife ; and on several such occasions he made an effort to take an affectionate tone with her. But the unnatural sound of his voice each time only accentuated to himself the depth of his repugnance, while the hysterical promptness of her answers, the servile gratitude which trembled in her voice and shone out of her radiant face would, at such instances, make him breathless with rage. Poor Gitl! she strained every effort to please him ; she tried to charm him by all the simple-minded little coquetries she knew, by every art which her artless brain could invent ; and only succeeded in making herself more offensive than ever.

As to Jake's feelings for Joey, they now alternated between periods of indifference and gusts of exaggerated affection ; while, in some instances, when the boy let himself be fondled by his mother or returned her caresses in his childish way, he would appear to Jake as siding with his enemy, and share with Gitl his father's odium.

One afternoon, shortly after Jake's interview with Mamie in front of the Chrystie Street tenement house, Fanny called on Gitl.

"Are you Mrs. Podkovnik?" she inquired, with an embarrassed air.

"Yes; why?" Mrs. Podkovnik replied, turning pale. "She is come to tell me that Jake has eloped with that Polish girl," flashed upon her overwrought mind. At the same moment Fanny, sizing her up, exclaimed inwardly, "So this is the kind of woman she is, poor thing!"

"Nothing. I *just* want to speak to you," the visitor uttered, mysteriously.

"What is it?"

"As I say, nothing at all. Is there nobody else in the house?" Fanny demanded, looking about.

"May I not live till to-morrow if there is a living soul except my boy, and he is asleep.

You may speak; never fear. But first tell me who you are; do not take ill my question. Be seated."

The girl's appearance and manner began to inspire Gitl with confidence.

"My name is Rosy—Rosy Blank," said Fanny, as she took a seat on the further end of the lounge. "'*F cou'se*, you don't know me, how should you? But I know you well enough, never mind that we have never seen each other before. I used to work with your husband in one shop. I have come to tell you such an important thing! You must know it. It makes no difference that you don't know who I am. May God grant me as good a year as my friendship is for you."

"Something about Jake?" Gitl blurted out, all anxiety, and instantly regretted the question.

"How did you guess? About Jake it is! About him and somebody else. But see how you did guess! Swear that you won't tell anybody that I have been here."

"May I be left speechless, may my arms
and legs be paralyzed, if I ever say a word!"
Gitl recited vehemently, thrilling with anxiety and impatience. "So it is! they have
eloped!" she added in her heart, seating herself close to her caller. "A darkness upon
my years! What will become of me and
Yosselé now?"

"Remember, now, not a word, either to
Jake or to anybody else in the world. I had
a mountain of *trouble* before I found out
where you lived, and I *stopped* work on purpose to come and speak to you. As true as
you see me alive. I wanted to call when
I was sure to find you alone, you understand. Is there really nobody about?" And
after a preliminary glance at the door and
exacting another oath of discretion from
Mrs. Podkovnik, Fanny began in an undertone:

"There is a girl; well, her name is Mamie; well, she and your husband used to go
to the same dancing school—that is a place
where *fellers* and *ladies* learn to dance," she

explained. "I go there, too; but I know your husband from the shop."

"But that *lada* has also worked in the same shop with him, hasn't she?" Gitl broke in, with a desolate look in her eye.

"Why, did Jake tell you she had?" Fanny asked in surprise.

"No, not at all, not at all! I am just asking. May I be sick if I know anything."

"The idea! How could they work together, seeing that she is a shirtmaker and he a cloakmaker. Ah, if you knew what a witch she is! She has set her mind on your husband, and is bound to take him away from you. She hitched on to him long ago. But since you came I thought she would have God in her heart, and be ashamed of people. Not she! She be ashamed! You may sling a cat into her face and she won't mind it. The black year knows where she grew up. I tell you there is not a girl in the whole dancing school but can not bear the sight of that Polish lizard!"

"Why, do they meet and kiss?" Gitl

moaned out. "Tell me, do tell me all, my little crown, keep nothing from me, tell me my whole dark lot."

"*Ull right*, but be sure not to speak to anybody. I'll tell you the truth: My name is not Rosy Blank at all. It is Fanny Scutelsky. You see, I am telling you the whole truth. The other evening they stood near the house where she *boards*, on Chrystie Street; so they were looking into each other's eyes and talking like a pair of little doves. A *lady* who is a *particla* friend of mine saw them; so she says a child could have guessed that she was making love to him and *trying* to get him away from you. '*F cou'se* it is none of my *business*. Is it my *business*, then? What do *I* care? It is only *becuss* I pity you. It is like the nature I have; I can not bear to see anybody in trouble. Other people would not *care*, but I do. Such is my nature. So I thought to myself I must go and tell Mrs. Podkovnik all about it, in order that she might know what to do."

For several moments Gitl sat speechless,
her head hung down, and her bosom heaving
rapidly.   Then she fell to swaying her frame
sidewise,   and   vehemently   wringing   her
hands.

"*Oi!   Oi!* Little mother! A pain to
me!" she moaned. "What is to be done?
Lord of the world, what is to be done?
Come to the rescue!   People, do take pity,
come to the rescue!"   She broke into a fit
of low sobbing, which shook her whole form
and was followed by a torrent of tears.

Whereupon Fanny also burst out crying,
and falling upon Gitl's shoulder she murmured: "My little heart! you don't know
what a friend I am to you! Oh, if you
knew what a serpent that Polish thief is!"

CHAPTER VII.

MRS. KAVARSKY'S COUP D'ÉTAT.

IT was not until after supper time that
Gitl could see Mrs. Kavarsky; for the neighbour's husband was in the installment business, and she generally spent all day in help-
ing him with his collections as well as
canvassing for new customers. When Gitl
came in to unburden herself of Fanny's rev-
elations, she found her confidante out of
sorts. Something had gone wrong in Mrs.
Kavarsky's affairs, and, while she was per-
fectly aware that she had only herself to
blame, she had laid it all to her husband and
had nagged him out of the house before he
had quite finished his supper.

She listened to her neighbour's story

with a bored and impatient air, and when
Gitl had concluded and paused for her opinion, she remarked languidly : " It serves you
right ! It is all *becuss* you will not throw
away that ugly kerchief of yours. What is
the use of your asking my advice ? "

" *Oi !* I think even that wouldn't help it
now," Gitl rejoined, forlornly. " The Uppermost knows what drug she has charmed him
with. A cholera into her, Lord of the
world ! " she added, fiercely.

Mrs. Kavarsky lost her temper.

" *Say*, will you stop talking nonsense ? "
she shouted savagely. " No wonder your
husband does not *care* for you, seeing these
stupid greenhornlike notions of yours."

" How then could she have bewitched
him, the witch that she is ? Tell me, little
heart, little crown, do tell me ! Take pity
and be a mother to me. I am so lonely
and ——" Heartrending sobs choked her
voice.

" What shall I tell you ? that you are a
blockhead ? *Oi ! Oi ! Oi !* " she mocked her.

"Will the crying help you? *Ull right*, cry away!"

"But what shall I do?" Gitl pleaded, wiping her tears. "It may drive me mad. I won't wear the kerchief any more. I swear this is the last day," she added, propitiatingly.

"*Dot's right!* When you talk like a man I like you. And now sit still and listen to what an older person and a business woman has to tell you. In the first place, who knows what that girl—Jennie, Fannie, Shmennie, Yomtzedemennie—whatever you may call her—is after?" The last two names Mrs. Kavarsky invented by poetical license to complete the rhyme and for the greater emphasis of her contempt. "In the second place, *asposel* [supposing] he did talk to that Polish piece of disturbance. *Vell*, what of it? It is all over with the world, isn't it? The mourner's prayer is to be said after it, I declare! A married man stood talking to a girl! Just think of it! May no greater evil befall any Yiddish daughter. This is

not Europe where one dares not say a word
to a strange woman! *Nu, sir!*"

"What, then, is the matter with him?
At home he would hardly ever leave my
side, and never ceased looking into my eyes.
Woe is me, what America has brought me
to!" And again her grief broke out into a
flood of tears.

This time Mrs. Kavarsky was moved.

"Don't be crying, my child; he may
come in for you," she said, affectionately.
"Believe me you are making a mountain out
of a fly—you are imagining too much."

"*Oi*, as my ill luck would have it, it is
all but too true. Have I no eyes, then?
He mocks at everything I say or do; he can
not bear the touch of my hand. America
has made a mountain of ashes out of me.
Really, a curse upon Columbus!" she ejaculated mournfully, quoting in all earnestness a
current joke of the Ghetto.

Mrs. Kavarsky was too deeply touched
to laugh. She proceeded to examine her
pupil, in whispers, upon certain details, and

10

thereupon her interest in Gitl's answers gradually superseded her commiseration for the
unhappy woman.

"And how does he behave toward the
boy?" she absently inquired, after a melancholy pause.

"Would he were as kind to me!"

"Then it is *all right!* Such things will
happen between man and wife. It is all
humbuk. It will all come right, and you
will some day be the happiest woman in the
world. You shall see. Remember that
Mrs. Kavarsky has told you so. And in the
meantime stop crying. A husband hates a
sniveller for a wife. You know the story of
Jacob and Leah, as it stands written in the
Holy Five Books, don't you? Her eyes became red with weeping, and Jacob, our father, did not *care* for her on that account.
Do you understand?"

All at once Mrs. Kavarsky bit her lip,
her countenance brightening up with a sudden inspiration. At the next instant she
made a lunge at Gitl's head, and off went the

kerchief. Gitl started with a cry, at the same moment covering her head with both hands.

"Take off your hands! Take them off at once, I say!" the other shrieked, her eyes flashing fire and her feet performing an Irish jig.

Gitl obeyed for sheer terror. Then, pushing her toward the sink, Mrs. Kavarsky said peremptorily : "You shall wash off your silly tears and I'll arrange your hair, and from this day on there shall be no kerchief, do you hear?"

Gitl offered but feeble resistance, just enough to set herself right before her own conscience. She washed herself quietly, and when her friend set about combing her hair, she submitted to the operation without a murmur, save for uttering a painful hiss each time there came a particularly violent tug at the comb; for, indeed, Mrs. Kavarsky plied her weapon rather energetically and with a bloodthirsty air, as if inflicting punishment. And while she was thus attacking

Gitl's luxurious raven locks she kept growling, as glibly as the progress of the comb would allow, and modulating her voice to its movements: " Believe me you are a lump of hunchback, *sure ;* you may—may depend up-upon it! Tell me, now, do you ever comb yourself? You have raised quite a plica, the black year take it! Another woman would thank God for such beau-beautiful hair, and here she keeps it hidden and makes a bu-bugbear of herself—a *regele monkey !* " she concluded, gnashing her teeth at the stout resistance with which her implement was at that moment grappling.

Gitl's heart swelled with delight, but she modestly kept silent.

Suddenly Mrs. Kavarsky paused thoughtfully, as if conceiving a new idea. In another moment a pair of scissors and curling irons appeared on the scene. At the sight of this Gitl's blood ran chill, and when the scissors gave their first click in her hair she felt as though her heart snapped. Nevertheless, she endured it all without a protest, blindly trusting that these instruments of torture would help ‚reinstall her in Jake's good graces.

At last, when all was ready and she found herself adorned with a pair of rich side bangs, she was taken in front of the mirror, and ordered to hail the transformation with joy. She viewed herself with an unsteady glance, as if her own face struck her as unfamiliar and forbidding. However, the change pleased her as much as it startled her.

" Do you really think he will like it ? " she inquired with piteous eagerness, in a fever of conflicting emotions.

" If he does not, I shall refund your money ! " her guardian snarled, in high glee.

For a moment or so Mrs. Kavarsky paused to admire the effect of her art. Then, in a sudden transport of enthusiasm, she sprang upon her ward, and with an " *Oi*, a health to you ! " she smacked a hearty kiss on her burning cheek.

"And now come, piece of wretch ! " So saying, Mrs. Kavarsky grasped Gitl by the

wrist, and forcibly convoyed her into her
husband's presence.

The two boarders were out, Jake being
alone with Joey.   He was seated at the table, facing the door, with the boy on his
knees.

"*Goot-evenik*, Mr. Podkovnik! Look
what I have brought you: a brand new
wife!" Mrs. Kavarsky said, pointing at her
charge, who stood faintly struggling to dis-
engage her hand from her escort's tight grip,
her eyes looking to the ground and her
cheeks a vivid crimson.

Gitl's unwonted appearance impressed
Jake as something unseemly and meretri-
cious.   The sight of her revolted him.

"It becomes her like a—a—a wet cat," he
faltered out with a venomous smile, choking
down a much stronger simile which would
have conveyed his impression with much
more precision, but which he dared not apply to his own wife.

The boy's first impulse upon the entrance of his mother had been to run up to her side and to greet her merrily; but he, too, was shocked by the change in her aspect, and he remained where he was, looking from her to Jake in blank surprise.

"Go away, you don't mean it!" Mrs. Kavarsky remonstrated distressedly, at the same moment releasing her prisoner, who forthwith dived into the bedroom to bury her face in a pillow, and to give way to a stream of tears. Then she made a few steps toward Jake, and speaking in an undertone she proceeded to take him to task. "Another man would consider himself happy to have such a wife," she said. "Such a quiet, honest woman! And such a housewife! Why, look at the way she keeps everything—like a fiddle. It is simply a treat to come into your house. I do declare you sin!"

"What do I do to her?" he protested morosely, cursing the intruder in his heart.

"Who says you do? Mercy and peace! Only—you understand—how shall I say it? —she is only a young woman; *vell*, so she

imagines that you do not *care* for her as much
as you used to. Come, Mr. Podkovnik, you
know you are a sensible man! I have always thought you one—you may ask my
husband. Really you ought.to be ashamed
of yourself. A prohibition upon me if I
could ever have believed it of you. Do you
think a stylish girl would make you a better
wife? If you do, you are grievously mistaken. What are they good for, the hus-
sies? To darken the life of a husband?
That, I admit, they are really great hands at.
They only know how to squander his money
for a new hat or rag every Monday and
Thursday, and to tramp around with other
men, fie upon the abominations! May no
good Jew know them!"

Her innuendo struck Mrs. Kavarsky as
extremely ingenious, and, egged on by the
dogged silence of her auditor, she ventured a
step further.

"Do you mean to tell me," she went on,
emphasizing each word, and shaking her
whole body with melodramatic defiance,

"that you would be better off with a *dantz-in'-school* girl?"

"*A danshin'-shchool* girl?" Jake repeat-ed, turning ashen pale, and fixing his inquisi-tress with a distant gaze. "Who says I care for a danshin'-shchool girl?" he bellowed, as he let down the boy and started to his feet red as a cockscomb. "It was she who told you that, was it?"

Joey had tripped up to the lounge where he now stood watching his father with a stare in which there was more curiosity than fright.

The little woman lowered her crest. "Not at all! God be with you!" she said quickly, in a tone of abject cowardice, and in-voluntarily shrinking before the ferocious at-titude of Jake's strapping figure. "Who? What? When? I did not mean anything at all, *sure.* Gitl *never* said a word to me. A prohibition if she did. Come, Mr. Pod-kovnik, why should you get *ektzited?*" she pursued, beginning to recover her presence of mind. "By-the-bye—I came near forget-

ting—how about the boarder you promised
to get me; do you remember, Mr. Podkovnik?"

"Talk away a toothache for your grandma, not for me. Who told her about *danshin'* girls?" he thundered again, re-enforcing
the ejaculation with an English oath, and
bringing down a violent fist on the table as
he did so.

At this Gitl's sobs made themselves heard
from the bedroom. They lashed Jake into a
still greater fury.

"What is she whimpering about, the
piece of stench! *Alla right*, I do hate her;
I can not bear the sight of her; and let her
do what she likes. *I don' care!*"

"Mr. Podkovnik! To think of a *sma't*
man like you talking in this way!"

"Dot'sh alla right!" he said, somewhat re-
lenting. "I don't *care* for any *danshin'* girls.
It is a —— —— lie! It was that scabby
greenhorn who must have taken it into her
head. I don't *care* for anybody; not for her
certainly"—pointing to the bedroom. "I/

am an *American feller*, a *Yankee*—that's
what I am. What punishment is due to me,
then, if I can not stand a *shnooza* like her?
It is *nu ushcd;* I can not live with her, even
if she stand one foot on heaven and one on
earth.   Let her take everything"—with a
wave at the household effects—"and I shall
pay her as much *cash* as she asks—I am
willing to break stones to pay her—provided
she agrees to a divorce."

The word had no sooner left his lips than
Gitl burst out of the darkness of her retreat,
her bangs dishevelled, her face stained and
flushed with weeping and rage, and her eyes,
still suffused with tears, flashing fire.

"May you and your Polish harlot be
jumping out of your skins and chafing with
wounds as long as you will have to wait for
a divorce!" she exploded. "He thinks I
don't know how they stand together near
her house making love to each other!"

Her unprecedented show of pugnacity
took him aback.

"Look at the Cossack of straw!" he said

quietly, with a forced smile. "Such a piece of cholera!" he added, as if speaking to himself, as he resumed his seat. "I wonder who tells her all these fibs?"

Gitl broke into a fresh flood of tears.

"*Vell*, what do you want now?" Mrs. Kavarsky said, addressing herself to her. "He says it is a lie. I told you you take all sorts of silly notions into your head."

"*Ach*, would it were a lie!" Gitl answered between her sobs.

At this juncture the boy stepped up to his mother's side, and nestled against her skirt. She clasped his head with both her hands, as though gratefully accepting an offer of succour against an assailant. And then, for the vague purpose of wounding Jake's feelings, she took the child in her arms, and huddling him close to her bosom, she half turned from her husband, as much as to say, "We two are making common cause against you." Jake was cut to the quick. He kept his glance fixed on the reddened, tear-stained profile of her nose, and, choking with hate,

he was going to say, "For my part, hang
yourself together with him!" But he had
self - mastery enough to repress the exclamation, confining himself to a disdainful
smile.

"Children, children! Woe, how you do
sin!" Mrs. Kavarsky sermonized. "Come
now, obey an older person. Whoever takes
notice of such trifles? You have had a
quarrel? *ull right!* And now make peace.
Have an embrace and a good kiss and *dot's
ull! Hurry yup*, Mr. Podkovnik! Don't
be ashamed!" she beckoned to him, her
countenance wreathed in voluptuous smiles
in anticipation of the love scene about to en-
act itself before her eyes. Mr. Podkovnik
failing to hurry up, however, she went on
disappointedly: "Why, Mr. Podkovnik!
Look at the boy the Uppermost has given
you. Would he might send me one like
him. Really, you ought to be ashamed of
yourself."

"Vot you kickin' aboyt, anyhoy?" Jake
suddenly fired out, in English. "Min' jou

on businesh an' dot'sh ull,'' he added indig-
nantly, averting his head.

Mrs. Kavarsky grew as red as a boiled
lobster.

"Vo—vo—vot *you* kecck aboyt?" she
panted, drawing herself up and putting her
arms akimbo. "He must think I, too, can
be scared by his English. I declare my shirt
has turned linen for fright! I was in America while you were hauling away at the bellows in Povodye; do you know it?"

"Are you going out of my house or
not?" roared Jake, jumping to his feet.

"And if I am not, what will you do?
Will you call a *politzman? Ull right*, do.
That is just what I want. I shall tell him I
can not leave her alone with a murderer like
you, for fear you might kill her and the boy,
so that you might dawdle around with that
Polish wench of yours. Here you have it!"
Saying which, she put her thumb between
her index and third finger—the Russian
version of the well-known gesture of contempt — presenting it to her adversary

together with a generous portion of her
tongue.

Jake's first impulse was to strike the
meddlesome woman. As he started toward
her, however, he changed his mind. "*Alla
right*, you may remain with her!" he said,
rushing up to the clothes rack, and slipping
on his coat and hat. "*Alla right*," he repeated with broken breath, "we shall see!"
And with a frantic bang of the door he dis-
appeared.

The fresh autumn air of the street at
once produced its salutary effect on his over-
excited nerves. As he grew more collected
he felt himself in a most awkward muddle.
He cursed his outbreak of temper, and
wished the next few days were over and the
breach healed. In his abject misery he
thought of suicide, of fleeing to Chicago or
St. Louis, all of which passed through his
mind in a stream of the most irrelevant and
the most frivolous reminiscences. He was
burning to go back, but the nerve failing

him to face Mrs.. Kavarsky, he wondered
where he was going to pass the night. It
was too cold to bé tramping about till it was
time to go to work, and he had not change
enough to pay for a night's rest in a lodging
house; so in his despair he fulminated
against Gitl and, above all, against her tu-
toress. Having passed as far as the limits
of the Ghetto he took a homeward course
by a parallel street, knowing all the while
that he would lack the courage to enter his
house. When he came within sight of it he
again turned back, yearningly thinking of
the cosey little home behind him, and invok-
ing maledictions upon Gitl for enjoying it
now while he was exposed to the chill air
without the prospect of shelter for the night.
As he thus sauntered reluctantly about he
meditated upon the scenes coming in his
way, and upon the thousand and one things
which they brought to his mind. At the
same time his heart was thirsting for Mamie,
and he felt himself a wretched outcast, the
target of ridicule—a martyr paying the pen-

alty of sins, which he failed to recognise as sins, or of which, at any rate, he could not hold himself culpable.

Yes, he will go to Chicago, or to Baltimore, or, better still, to England. He pictured to himself the sensation it would produce and Gitl's despair. " It will serve her right. What does she want of me ? " he said to himself, revelling in a sense of revenge. But then it was such a pity to part with Joey! Whereupon, in his reverie, Jake beheld himself stealing into his house in the dead of night, and kidnapping the boy. And what would Mamie say? Would she not be sorry to have him disappear? Can it be that she does not care for him any longer? She seemed to. But that was before she knew him to be a married man. And again his heart uttered curses against Gitl. Ah, if Mamie did still care for him, and fainted upon hearing of his flight, and then could not sleep, and ran around wringing her hands and raving like mad! It would serve *her* right, too! She should

have come to tell him she loved him instead
of making that scene at his house and taking a derisive tone with him upon the occasion of his visit to her. Still, should she
come to join him in London, he would receive her, he decided magnanimously. They
speak English in London, and have cloak
shops like here. So he would be no greenhorn there, and wouldn't they be happy—he,
Mamie, and little Joey! Or, supposing his
wife suddenly died, so that he could legally
marry Mamie and remain in New York——

A mad desire took hold of him to see
the Polish girl, and he involuntarily took the
way to her lodging. What is he going to
say to her? Well, he will beg her not to be
angry for his failure to pay his debt, take her
into his confidence on the subject of his proposed flight, and promise to send her every
cent from London. And while he was per-
fectly aware that he had neither the money
to take him across the Atlantic nor the heart
to forsake Gitl and Joey, and that Mamie
would never let him leave New York with-

out paying her twenty-five dollars, he started out on a run in the direction of Chrystie Street. Would she might offer to join him in his flight! She must have money enough for two passage tickets, the rogue. Wouldn't it be nice to be with her on the steamer! he thought, as he wrathfully brushed apart a group of street urchins impeding his way..

CHAPTER VIII.

A HOUSETOP IDYL.

JAKE found Mamie on the sidewalk in front of the tenement house where she lodged. As he came rushing up to her side, she was pensively rehearsing a waltz step.

"Mamie, come shomeversh! I got to shpeak to you a lot," he gasped out.

"Vot's de madder?" she demanded, startled by his excited manner.

"This is not the place for speaking," he rejoined vehemently, in Yiddish. "Let us go to the Grand Street dock or to Seventh Street park. There we can speak so that nobody overhears us."

"I bet you he is going to ask me to run away with him," she prophesied to herself;

158

and in her feverish impatience to hear him
out she proposed to go on the roof, which,
the evening being cool, she knew to be deserted.

When they reached the top of the house
they found it overhung with rows of half-
dried linen, held together with wooden
clothespins and trembling to the fresh autumn breeze. Overhead, fleecy clouds were
floating across a starry blue sky, now concealing and now exposing to view a pallid
crescent of new moon. Coming from the
street below there was a muffled, mysterious
hum ever and anon drowned in the clatter
and jingle of a passing horse car. A lurid,
exceedingly uncanny sort of idyl it was; and
in the midst of it there was something extremely weird and gruesome in those
stretches of wavering, fitfully silvered white,
to Jake's overtaxed mind vaguely suggesting
the burial clothes of the inmates of a Jewish
graveyard.

After picking and diving their way be-
neath the trembling lines of underwear, pil-

lowcases, sheets, and what not, they paused
in front of a tall chimney pot. Jake, in a
medley of superstitious terror, infatuation,
and bashfulness, was at a loss how to begin
and, indeed, what to say. Feeling that it
would be easy for him to break into tears he
instinctively chose this as the only way out
of his predicament.

" *Vot's de madder*, Jake? Speak out!"
she said, with motherly harshness.

He now wished to say something, although he still knew not what; but his sobs
once called into play were past his control.

"She must give you *trouble*," the girl
added softly, after a slight pause, her excitement growing with every moment.

"Ach, Mamielé!" he at length exclaimed,
resolutely wiping his tears with his handker-
chief. " My life has become so dark and bit-
ter to me, I might as well put a rope around
my neck."

" Does she eat you ? "

" Let her go to all lamentations! Somebody told her I go around with you."

"But you know it is a lie! Some one must have seen us the other evening when we were standing downstairs. You had better not come here, then. When you have some money, you will send it to me," she concluded, between genuine sympathy and an intention to draw him out.

"*Ach*, don't say that, Mamie. What is the good of my life without you? I don't sleep nights. Since she came I began to understand how dear you are to me. I can not tell it so well," he said, pointing to his heart.

" *Yes, but* before she came you didn't *care* for me!" she declared, labouring to disguise the exultation which made her heart dance.

" I always did, Mamie. May I drop from this roof and break hand and foot if I did not."

A flood of wan light struck Mamie full in her swarthy face, suffusing it with ivory effulgence, out of which her deep dark eyes gleamed with a kind of unearthly lustre.

Jake stood enravished. He took her by the hand, but she instantly withdrew it, edging away a step. His touch somehow restored her to calm self-possession, and even kindled a certain thirst for revenge in her heart.

" It is not what it used to be, Jake," she said in tones of complaisant earnestness. " Now that I know you are a married man it is all gone. *Yes*, Jake, it is all gone! You should have cared for me when she was still there. Then you could have gone to a rabbi and sent her a writ of divorce. It is too late now, Jake."

" It is not too late !" he protested, tremulously. " I will get a divorce, *anyhoy*. And if you don't take me I will hang myself," he added, imploringly.

" On a burned straw ?" she retorted, with a cruel chuckle.

" It is all very well for you to laugh. But if you could enter my heart and see how I *shuffer !* "

" Woe is me ! I don't see how you will stand it," she mocked him. And abruptly

assuming a grave tone, she pursued vehemently : " But I don't understand ; since you
sent her tickets and money, you must like
her."

Jake explained that he had all along
intended to send her rabbinical divorce papers instead of a passage ticket, and that it
had been his old mother who had pestered
him, with her tear-stained letters, into acting
contrary to his will.

" *All right*," Mamie resumed, with a
dubious smile ; " but why don't you go to
Fanny, or Beckie, or Beilké the " Black Cat " ?
You used to care for them more than for
me. Why should you just come to me ? "

- Jake answered by characterizing the girls
she had mentioned in terms rather too high-
scented for print, protesting his loathing for
them. Whereupon she subjected him to a
rigid cross-examination as to his past con-
duct toward herself and her rivals ; and although he managed to explain matters to
her inward satisfaction, owing, chiefly, to a
predisposition on her own part to credit his

assertions on the subject, she could not help continuing obdurate and in a spiteful, vindictive mood.

"All you say is not worth a penny, and it is too late, *anyvay*," was her verdict. "You have a wife and a child ; better go home and be a father to your *boy*." Her last words were uttered with some approach to sincerity, and she was mentally beginning to give herself credit for magnanimity and pious self-denial. She would have regretted her exhortation, however, had she been aware of its effect on her listener ; for her mention of the boy and appeal to Jake as a father aroused in him a lively sense of the wrong he was doing. Moreover, while she was speaking his attention had been attracted to a loosened pillowcase ominously fluttering and flapping a yard or two off. The figure of his dead father, attired in burial linen, uprose to his mind.

"You don' vanted ? Alla right, you be shorry," he said half-heartedly, turning to go.

"*Hol' on !*" she checked him, irritatedly.

" How are you going to *fix* it ? Are you
sure she will take a divorce ? "

" Will she have a choice then ? She will
have to take it. I won't live with her *anyhoy*," he replied, his passion once more well-
ing up in his soul. " Mamie, my treasure,
my glory ! " he exclaimed, in tremulous accents. " Say that you are *shatichfied;* my
heart will become lighter." Saying which, he
strained her to his bosom, and fell to raining
fervent kisses on her face. At first she made
a faint attempt at freeing herself, and then
suddenly clasping him with mad force she
pressed her lips to his in a fury of passion.

The pillowcase flapped aloud, ever more
sternly, warningly, portentously.

Jake cast an involuntary side glance at it.
His spell of passion was broken and sup-
planted by a spell of benumbing terror. He
had an impulse to withdraw his arms from
the girl ; but, instead, he clung to her all the
faster, as if for shelter from the ghostlike
thing.

With a last frantic hug Mamie relaxed

her hold. " Remember now, Jake ! " she then said, in a queer hollow voice. " Now it is all *settled.* Maybe you are making fun of me ? If you are, you are playing with fire. Death to me—death to you ! " she added, menacingly.

He wished to say something to reassure her, but his tongue seemed grown fast to his palate.

" Am I to blame ? " she continued with ghastly vehemence, sobs ringing in her voice. " Who asked you to come ? Did I lure you from her, then ? I should sooner have thrown myself into the river than taken away somebody else's husband. You say yourself that you would not live with her, *anyvay.* But now it is all gone. Just try to leave me now ! " And giving vent to her tears, she added, " Do you think my heart is no heart ? "

A thrill of joyous pity shot through his frame. Once again he caught her to his heart, and in a voice quivering with tender- ness he murmured : " Don't be uneasy, my

dear, my gold, my pearl, my consolation ! I
will let my throat be cut, into fire or water
will I go, for your sake."

" Dot's all right," she returned, musingly.
" But how are you going to get rid of her ?
You von't go back on me, vill you ? " she
asked in English.

" *Me ?* May I not be able to get away
from this spot. Can it be that you still dis-
trust me ? "

" Swear ! "

" How else shall I swear ? "

" By your father, peace upon him."

" May my father as surely have a bright
paradise," he said, with a show of alacrity, his
mind fixed on the loosened pillowcase.
" *Vell*, are you *shatichfied* now ? "

" All right," she answered, in a matter-of-
fact way, and as if only half satisfied. " But
do you think she will take money ? "

" But I have none."

" Nobody asks you if you have. But
would she take it, if you had ? "

" If I had ! I am sure she would take

it ; she would have to, for what would she
gain if she did not ? "

"Are you *sure ?* "

"*'F cush !* "

"*Ach*, but, after all, why did you not
tell me you liked me before she came ? " she
said testily, stamping her foot.

" Again !" he exclaimed, wincing.

" *All right ;* wait."

She turned to go somewhere, but
checked herself, and facing about, she ex-
acted an additional oath of allegiance. After which she went to the other side of the
chimney. When she returned she held one
of her arms behind her.

" You will not let yourself be talked
away from me ? "

He swore.

" Not even if your father came to you
from the other world—if he came to you in a
dream, I mean—and told you to drop me ? "

Again he swore.

" And you really don't care for Fanny ? "

And again he swore.

" Nor for Beckie ? "

The ordeal was too much, and he begged her to desist. But she wouldn't, and so, chafing under inexorable cross-examinations, he had to swear again and again that he had never cared for any of Joe's female pupils or assistants except Mamie.

At last she relented.

" Look, piece of loafer you ! " she then said, holding out an open bank book to his eyes. " But what is the *use ?* It is not light enough, and you can not read, *anyvay.* You can eat, *dot's all.* *Vell,* you could make out figures, couldn't you ? There are three hundred and forty dollars," she proceeded, pointing to the balance line, which represented the savings, for a marriage portion, of five years' hard toil. " It should be three hundred and sixty-five, but then for the twenty-five dollars you owe me I may as well light a mourner's candle, *ain' it ?* "

When she had started to produce the bank book from her bosom he had surmised her intent, and while she was gone he was

making guesses as to the magnitude of the
sum to her credit. His most liberal esti-
mate, however, had been a hundred and
fifty dollars; so that the revelation of the
actual figure completely overwhelmed him.
He listened to her with a broad grin, and
when she paused he burst out :

"Mamielé, you know what ? Let us run
away ! "

"You are a fool !" she overruled him,
as she tucked the bank book under her
jacket. "I have a better plan. But tell
me the truth, did you not guess I had
money ? Now you need not fear to tell me
all."

He swore that he had not even dreamt
that she possessed a bank account. How
could he ? And was it not because he had
suspected the existence of such an account
that he had come to declare his love to her
and not to Fanny, or Beckie, or the " Black
Cat "? No, may he be thunderstruck if it
was. What does she take him for ? On his
part she is free to give the money away or

throw it into the river. He will become a boss, and take her penniless, for he can not live without her ; she is lodged in his heart ; she is the only woman he ever cared for.

" Oh, but why did you not tell me all this long ago ? " With which, speaking like the complete mistress of the situation that she was, she proceeded to expound a project, which had shaped itself in her lovelorn mind, hypothetically, during the previous few days, when she had been writhing in despair of ever having an occasion to put it into practice. Jake was to take refuge with her married sister in Philadelphia until Gitl was brought to terms. In the meantime some chum of his, nominated by Mamie and acting under her orders, would carry on negotiations. The State divorce, as she had already taken pains to ascertain, would cost fifty dollars ; the rabbinical divorce would take five or eight dollars more. Two hundred dollars would be deposited with some Canal Street banker, to be paid to Gitl when the whole procedure was brought to a successful termination, If she can be got to accept less, so much the better; if not, Jake and Mamie will get along, anyhow. When they are married they will open a dancing school.

To all of which Jake kept nodding approval, once or twice interrupting her with a demonstration of enthusiasm. As to the fate of his boy, Mamie deliberately circumvented all reference to the subject. Several times Jake was tempted to declare his ardent desire to have the child with them, and that Mamie should like him and be a mother to him; for had she not herself found him a bright and nice fellow? His heart bled at the thought of having to part with Joey. But somehow the courage failed him to touch upon the question. He saw himself helplessly entangled in something foreboding no good. He felt between the devil and the deep sea, as the phrase goes; and unnerved by the whole situation and completely in the shop girl's power, he was glad to be relieved from all initiative—whether forward or backward—to shut his eyes, as it were, and, leaning upon Mamie's strong arm, let himself be led by her in whatever direction she chose.

"Do you know, Jake?—now I may as well tell you," the girl pursued, à propos of the prospective dancing school; "do you know that Joe has been *bodering* me to marry him? And he did not know I had a cent, either."

"*An' you didn' vanted?*" Jake asked, joyfully.

"*Sure!* I knew all along Jakie was my predestined match," she replied, drawing his bulky head to her lips. And following the operation by a sound twirl of his ear, she added: "Only he is a great lump of hog, Jakie is. But a heart is a clock: it told me I would have you some day. I could have got *lots* of suitors—may the two of us have as many thousands of dollars—and *business people*, too. Do you see what I am doing for you? Do you deserve it, *monkey you?*"

"*Never min'*, you shall see what a *danshin' shchool* I *shta't*. If I don't take away

every *shcholar* from Jaw, my name won't be
Jake. Won't he squirm!" he exclaimed, with
childish ardour.

"Dot's all right; but foist min' dot you
don' go back on me!"

An hour or two later Mamie with Jake
by her side stood in front of the little window in the ferryhouse of the Pennsylvania
Railroad, buying one ticket for the midnight
train for Philadelphia.

"Min' je, Jake," she said anxiously a little after, as she handed him the ticket.
"This is as good as a marriage certificate, do
you understand?" And the two hurried off
to the boat in a meagre stream of other passengers.

CHAPTER IX.

It was on a bright frosty morning in the following January, in the kitchen of Rabbi Aaronovitz, on the third floor of a rickety old tenement house, that Jake and Gitl, for the first time since his flight, came face to face. It was also to be their last meeting as husband and wife.

The low-ceiled room was fairly crowded with men and women. Besides the principal actors in the scene, the rabbi, the scribe, and the witnesses, and, as a matter of course, Mrs. Kavarsky, there was the rabbi's wife, their two children, and an envoy from Mamie, charged to look after the fortitude of Jake's nerve. Gitl, extremely careworn and

175

haggard, was "in her own hair," thatched with a broad-brimmed winter hat of a brown colour, and in a jacket of black beaver. The rustic, "greenhornlike" expression was completely gone from her face and manner, and, although she now looked bewildered and as if terror-stricken, there was noticeable about her a suggestion of that peculiar air of self-confidence with which a few months' life in America is sure to stamp the looks and bearing of every immigrant. Jake, flushed and plainly nervous and fidgety, made repeated attempts to conceal his state of mind now by screwing up a grim face, now by giving his enormous head a haughty posture, now by talking aloud to his escort.

The tedious preliminaries were as trying to the rabbi as they were to Jake and Gitl. However, the venerable old man discharged his duty of dissuading the young couple from their contemplated step as scrupulously as he dared in view of his wife's signals to desist and not to risk the fee. Gitl, prompted by Mrs. Kavarsky, responded to all ques-

tions with an air of dazed resignation, while
Jake, ever conscious of his guard's glance,
gave his answers with bravado. At last the
scribe, a gaunt middle-aged man, with an expression of countenance at once devout and
businesslike, set about his task. Whereupon Mrs. Aaronovitz heaved a sigh of relief,
and forthwith banished her two boys into
the parlour.

An imposing stillness fell over the room.
Little by little, however, it was broken, at
first by whispers and then by an unrestrained
hum. The rabbi, in a velvet skullcap, faded
and besprinkled with down, presided with
pious dignity, though apparently ill at ease,
at the head of the table. Alternately stroking his yellowish-gray beard and curling his
scanty side locks, he kept his eyes on the
open book before him, now and then stealing
a glance at the other end of the table, where
the scribe was rapturously drawing the
square characters of the holy tongue.

Gitl carefully looked away from Jake.
But he invincibly haunted her mind, render-

ing her deaf to Mrs. Kavarsky's incessant
buzz. His presence terrified her, and at the
same time it melted her soul in a fire, tortur-
ing yet sweet, which impelled her at one moment to throw herself upon him and scratch
out his eyes, and at another to prostrate herself at his feet and kiss them in a flood of
tears.

Jake, on the other hand, eyed Gitl quite
frequently, with a kind of malicious curiosity.
Her general Americanized make up, and,
above all, that broad-brimmed, rather fussy,
hat of hers, nettled him. It seemed to defy
him, and as if devised for that express purpose. Every time she and her adviser caught
his eye, a feeling of devouring hate for both
would rise in his heart. He was panting to
see his son; and, while he was thoroughly
alive to the impossibility of making a child
the witness of a divorce scene between father
and mother, yet, in his fury, he interpreted
their failure to bring Joey with them as another piece of malice.

" Ready !" the scribe at length called out,

getting up with the document in his hand, and turning it over to the rabbi.

The rest of the assemblage also rose from their seats, and clustered round Jake and Gitl, who had taken places on either side of the old man. A beam of hard, cold sunlight, filtering in through a grimy window-pane and falling lurid upon the rabbi's wrinkled brow, enhanced the impressiveness of the spectacle. A momentary pause ensued, stern, weird, and casting a spell of awe over most of the bystanders, not excluding the rabbi. Mrs. Kavarsky even gave a shudder and gulped down a sob.

"Young woman!" Rabbi Aaronovitz began, with bashful serenity, "here is the writ of divorce all ready. Now thou mayst still change thy mind."

Mrs. Aaronovitz anxiously watched Gitl, who answered by a shake of her head.

"Mind thee, I tell thee once again," the old man pursued, gently. "Thou must accept this divorce with the same free will and readiness with which thou hast married thy

husband. Should there be the slightest ob-
jection hidden in thy heart, the divorce is
null and void. Dost thou understand?"

"Say that you are *saresfied*," whispered
Mrs. Kavarsky.

"*Ull ride*, I am *salesfiet*," murmured Gitl,
looking down on the table.

"Witnesses, hear ye what this young
woman says? That she accepts the divorce
of her own free will," the rabbi exclaimed
solemnly, as if reading the Talmud.

"Then I must also tell you once more,"
he then addressed himself to Jake as well
as to Gitl, "that this divorce is good only
upon condition that you are also divorced by
the Government of the land—by the court—
do you understand? So it stands written in
the separate paper which you get. Do you
understand what I say?"

"*Dot'sh alla right*," Jake said, with ostentatious ease of manner. "I have already
told you that the *dvosh* of the *court* is already *fikshed*, haven't I?" he added, even
angrily.

Now came the culminating act of the drama. Gitl was affectionately urged to hold out her hands, bringing them together at an angle, so as to form a receptacle for the fateful piece of paper. - She obeyed mechanically, her cheeks turning ghastly pale. Jake, also pale to his lips, his brows contracted, received the paper, and obeying directions, approached the woman who in the eye of the Law of Moses was still his wife. And then, repeating word for word after the rabbi, he said :

" Here is thy divorce. Take thy divorce. And by this divorce thou art separated from me and free for all other men ! "

Gitl scarcely understood the meaning of the formula, though each Hebrew word was followed by its Yiddish translation. Her arms shook so that they had to be supported by Mrs. Kavarsky and by one of the witnesses.

At last Jake deposited the writ and instantly drew back.

Gitl closed her hands upon the paper as

she had been instructed; but at the same
moment she gave a violent tremble, and with
a heartrending groan fell on the witness in
a fainting swoon.

In the ensuing commotion Jake slipped
out of the room, presently followed by Mamie's ambassador, who had remained behind
to pay the bill.

Gitl was soon brought to by Mrs. Kavarsky and the mistress of the house. For
a moment or so she sat staring about her,
when, suddenly awakening to the meaning
of the ordeal she had just been through, and
finding Jake gone, she clapped her hands and
burst into a fit of sobbing.

Meanwhile the rabbi had once again pe-
rused the writ, and having caused the witnesses to do likewise, he made two diagonal
slits in the paper.

"You must not forget, my daughter," he
said to the young woman, who was at that
moment crying as if her heart would break,
"that you dare not marry again before nine-

ty-one days, counting from to-day, go by;
while you—where is he, the young man?
Gone?" he asked with a frustrated smile and
growing pale.

"You want him badly, don't you?"
growled Mrs. Kavarsky. "Let him go I
know where, the every-evil-in-him that he
is!"

Mrs. Aaronovitz telegraphing to her husband that the money was safe in her pocket,
he remarked sheepishly: "*He* may wed even
to-day." Whereupon Gitl's sobs became still
more violent, and she fell to nodding her
head and wringing her hands.

"What are you crying about, foolish face
that you are!" Mrs. Kavarsky fired out.
"Another woman would thank God for having at last got rid of the lump of leavened
bread. What say you, rabbi? A rowdy, a
sinner of Israel, a *regely loifer*, may no good
Jew know him! *Never min'*, the Name, be
It blessed, will send you your destined one,
and a fine, learned, respectable man, too," she
added significantly.

Her words had an instantaneous effect.
Gitl at once composed herself, and fell to
drying her eyes.

Quick to catch Mrs. Kavarsky's hint, the
rabbi's wife took her aside and asked eagerly:

" Why, has she got a suitor ? "

" What is the *differentz ?*   You need not
fear; when there is a wedding canopy I shall
employ no other man than your husband,"
was Mrs. Kavarsky's self-important but good-
natured reply.

CHAPTER X.

WHEN Gitl, accompanied by her friend, reached home, they were followed into the former's apartments by a batch of neighbours, one of them with Joey in tow. The moment the young woman found herself in her kitchen she collapsed, sinking down on the lounge. The room seemed to have assumed a novel aspect, which brought home to her afresh that the bond between her and Jake was now at last broken forever and beyond repair. The appalling fact was still further accentuated in her consciousness when she caught sight of the boy.

"Joeyelé! Joeyinké! Birdie! Little kitten!"—with which she seized him in her

arms, and, kissing him all over, burst into
tears. Then shaking with the child backward and forward, and intoning her words as
Jewish women do over a grave, she went on :
" Ai, you have no papa any more, Joeyelé !
Yoselé, little crown, you will never see him
again ! He is dead, *taté* is !" Whereupon
Yoselé, following his mother's example, let
loose his stentorian voice.

" *Shurr-r up !* " Mrs. Kavarsky whispered, stamping her foot. " You want Mr.
Bernstein to leave you, too, do you ? No
more is wanted than that he should get wind
of your crying."

" Nobody will tell him," one of the neighbours put in, resentfully. " But, *anyhull*,
what is the *used* crying ? "

" Ask her, the piece of hunchback ! " said
Mrs. Kavarsky. " Another woman would
dance for joy, and here she is whining, the
cudgel. What is it you are snivelling about ?
That you have got rid of an unclean bone
and a dunce, and that you are going to
marry a young man of silk who is fit to be a

rabbi, and is as *smart* and *ejecate* as a lawyer?
You would have got a match like that in
Povodye, would you? I dare say a man like
Mr. Bernstein would not have spoken to you
there. You ought to say Psalms for your
coming to America. It is only here that it
is possible for a blacksmith's wife to marry
a learned man, who is a blessing both for
God and people. And yet you are not
saresfied! Cry away! If Bernstein refuses
to go under the wedding canopy, Mrs.
Kavarsky will no more *bodder* her head
about you, depend upon it. It is not
enough for her that I neglect *business* on her
account," she appealed to the bystanders.

"Really, what are you crying about, Mrs.
Podkovnik?" one of the neighbours interposed. "You ought to bless the hour when
you became free."

All of which haranguing only served to
stimulate Gitl's demonstration of grief.
Having let down the boy, she went on clapping her hands, swaying in all directions, and
wailing.

13

The truth must be told, however, that
she was now continuing her lamentations by
the mere force of inertia, and as if enjoying
the very process of the thing. For, indeed,
at the bottom of her heart she felt herself far
from desolate, being conscious of the existence of a man who was to take care of her
and her child, and even relishing the prospect of the new life in store for her. Already on her way from the rabbi's house,
while her soul was full of Jake and the Polish girl, there had fluttered through her imagination a picture of the grocery business
which she and Bernstein were to start with
the money paid to her by Jake.

.   .   .   .

While Gitl thus sat swaying and wringing her hands, Jake, Mamie, her emissary at
the divorce proceeding, and another mutual
friend, were passengers on a Third Avenue
cable car, all bound for the mayor's office.
While Gitl was indulging herself in an exhibition of grief, her recent husband was flaunt-
ing a hilarious mood. He did feel a great

burden to have rolled off his heart, and the
proximity of Mamie, on the other hand, ca-
ressed his soul. He was tempted to catch
her in his arms, and cover her glowing cheeks
with kisses. But in his inmost heart he. was
the reverse of eager to reach the City Hall.
He was painfully reluctant to part with his
long-coveted freedom so soon after it had at
last been attained, and before he had had time
to relish it. Still worse than this thirst for a
taste of liberty was a feeling which was now
gaining upon him, that, instead of a con-
queror, he had emerged from the rabbi's
house the victim of an ignominious defeat.
If he could now have seen Gitl in her paroxysm of anguish, his heart would perhaps
have swelled with a sense of his triumph, and·
Mamie would have appeared to him the em-
bodiment of his future happiness. Instead
of this he beheld her, Bernstein, Yoselé, and
Mrs. Kavarsky celebrating their victory and
bandying jokes at his expense. ·Their future
seemed bright with joy, while his own
loomed dark and impenetrable. What if he

should now dash into Gitl's apartments and, declaring his authority as husband, father, and lord of the house, fiercely eject the strangers, take Yoselé in his arms, and sternly command Gitl to mind her household duties?

But the distance between him and the mayor's office was dwindling fast. Each time the car came to a halt he wished the pause could be prolonged indefinitely ; and when it resumed its progress, the violent lurch it gave was accompanied by a corresponding sensation in his heart.

THE END.

" A better book than ' The Prisoner of Zenda.' "—London Queen.

THE CHRONICLES OF COUNT ANTONIO.

By ANTHONY HOPE, author of " The God in the Car," " The Prisoner of Zenda," etc. With photogravure Frontispiece by S. W. Van Schaick. Third edition. 12mo. Cloth, $1.50.

" No adventures were ever better worth recounting than are those of Antonio of Monte Velluto, a very Bayard among outlaws. . . . To all those whose pulses still stir at the recital of deeds of high courage, we may recommend this book. . . . The chronicle conveys the emotion of heroic adventure, and is picturesquely written."—*London Daily News.*

" It has literary merits all its own, of a deliberate and rather deep order. . . . In point of execution ' The Chronicles of Count Antonio' is the best work that Mr. Hope has yet done. The design is clearer, the workmanship more elaborate, the style more colored. . . . The incidents are most ingenious, they are told quietly, but with great cunning, and the Quixotic sentiment which pervades it all is exceedingly pleasant."—*Westminster Gazette.*

" A romance worthy of all the expectations raised by the brilliancy of his former books, and likely to be read with a keen enjoyment and a healthy exaltation of the spirits by every one who takes it up."—*The Scotsman.*

" A gallant tale, written with unfailing freshness and spirit."—*London Daily Telegraph.*

" One of the most fascinating romances written in English within many days. The quaint simplicity of its style is delightful, and the adventures recorded in these ' Chronicles of Count Antonio' are as stirring and ingenious as any conceived even by Weyman at his best."—*New York World.*

" Romance of the real flavor, wholly and entirely romance, and narrated in true romantic style. The characters, drawn with such masterly handling, are not merely pictures and portraits, but statues that are alive and step boldly forward from the canvas."—*Boston Courier.*

" Told in a wonderfully simple and direct style, and with the magic touch of a man who has the genius of narrative, making the varied incidents flow naturally and rapidly in a stream of sparkling discourse."—*Detroit Tribune.*

" Easily ranks with, if not above, ' A Prisoner of Zenda.' . . . Wonderfully strong, graphic, and compels the interest of the most *blasé* novel reader."—*Boston Advertiser.*

" No adventures were ever better worth telling than those of Count Antonio. . . . The author knows full well how to make every pulse thrill, and how to hold his readers under the spell of his magic."—*Boston Herald.*

" A book to make women weep proud tears, and the blood of men to tingle with knightly fervor. . . . In ' Count Antonio ' we think Mr. Hope surpasses himself, as he has already surpassed all the other story-tellers of the period."—*New York Spirit of the Times.*

A JOURNEY IN OTHER WORLDS. A Ro-
mance of the Future. By JOHN JACOB ASTOR. With 9 full-
page Illustrations by Dan Beard. 12mo. Cloth, $1.50.

"An interesting and cleverly devised book. . . . No lack of imagination. . . .
Shows a skillful and wide acquaintance with scientific facts."—*New York Herald.*

"The author speculates cleverly and daringly on the scientific advance of the earth,
and he revels in the physical luxuriance of Jupiter; but he also lets his imagination
travel through spiritual realms, and evidently delights in mystic speculation quite as
much as in scientific investigation. If he is a follower of Jules Verne, he has not forgotten also to study the philosophers."—*New York Tribune.*

"A beautiful example of typographical art and the bookmaker's skill. . . . To
appreciate the story one must read it."—*New York Commercial Advertiser.*

"The date of the events narrated in this book is supposed to be 2000 A. D. The
inhabitants of North America have increased mightily in numbers and power and
knowledge. It is an age of marvelous scientific attainments. Flying machines have
long been in common use, and finally a new power is discovered called 'apergy,'
the reverse of gravitation, by which people are able to fly off into space in any direction, and at what speed they please."—*New York Sun.*

"The scientific romance by John Jacob Astor is more than likely to secure a distinct popular success, and achieve widespread vogue both as an amusing and interesting story, and a thoughtful endeavor to prophesy some of the triumphs which science
is destined to win by the year 2000. The book has been written with a purpose, and
that a higher one than the mere spinning of a highly imaginative yarn. Mr. Astor has
been engaged upon the book for over two years, and has brought to bear upon it a
great deal of hard work in the way of scientific research, of which he has been very fond
ever since he entered Harvard. It is admirably illustrated by Dan Beard."—*Mail and
Express.*

"Mr. Astor has himself almost all the qualities imaginable for making the science of
astronomy popular. He knows the learned maps of the astrologers. He knows the
work of Copernicus. He has made calculations and observations. He is enthusiastic,
and the spectacular does not frighten him."—*New York Times.*

"The work will remind the reader very much of Jules Verne in its general plan of
using scientific facts and speculation as a skeleton on which to hang the romantic
adventures of the central figures, who have all the daring ingenuity and luck of Mr.
Verne's heroes. Mr. Astor uses history to point out what in his opinion science may
be expected to accomplish. It is a romance with a purpose."—*Chicago Inter-Ocean.*

"The romance contains many new and striking developments of the possibilities
of science hereafter to be explored, but the volume is intensely interesting, both as a
product of imagination and an illustration of the ingenious and original application of
science."—*Rochester Herald.*

New York: D. APPLETON & CO., 72 Fifth Avenue.

D. APPLETON & CO.'S PUBLICATIONS.

THE STORY OF THE WEST SERIES.
EDITED BY RIPLEY HITCHCOCK.

"There is a vast extent of territory lying between the Missouri River and the Pacific coast which has barely been skimmed over so far. That the conditions of life therein are undergoing changes little short of marvelous will be understood when one recalls the fact that the first white male child born in Kansas is still living there; and Kansas is by no means one of the newer States. Revolutionary indeed has been the upturning of the old condition of affairs, and little remains thereof, and less will remain as each year goes by, until presently there will be only tradition of the Sioux and Comanches, the cowboy life, the wild horse, and the antelope. Histories, many of them, have been written about the Western country alluded to, but most if not practically all by outsiders who knew not personally that life of kaleidoscopic allurement. But ere it shall have vanished forever we are likely to have truthful, complete, and charming portrayals of it produced by men who actually know the life and have the power to describe it."— *Henry Edward Rood, in The Mail and Express.*

NOW READY.

*T*HE STORY OF THE INDIAN. By GEORGE BIRD GRINNELL, author of "Pawnee Hero Stories," "Blackfoot Lodge Tales," etc. 12mo. Cloth. Illustrated. $1.50.

"A valuable study of Indian life and character. . . . An attractive book, . . . in large part one in which Indians themselves might have written."—*New York Tribune.*

"Among the various books respecting the aborigines of America, Mr. Grinnell's easily takes a leading position. He takes the reader directly to the camp-fire and the council, and shows us the American Indian as he really is. . . . A book which will convey much interesting knowledge respecting a race which is now fast passing away."—*Boston Commercial Bulletin.*

"It must not be supposed that the volume is one only for scholars and libraries of reference. It is far more than that. While it is a true story, yet it is a story none the less abounding in picturesque description and charming anecdote. We regard it as a valuable contribution to American literature."—*N. Y. Mail and Express.*

"A most attractive book, which presents an admirable graphic picture of the actual Indian, whose home life, religious observances, amusements, together with the various phases of his devotion to war and the chase, and finally the effects of encroaching civilization, are delineated with a certainty and an absence of sentimentalism or hostile prejudice that impart a peculiar distinction to this eloquent story of a passing life."—*Buffalo Commercial.*

"No man is better qualified than Mr. Grinnell to introduce this series with the story of the original owner of the West, the North American Indian. Long acquaintance and association with the Indians, and membership in a tribe, combined with a high degree of literary ability and thorough education, has fitted the author to understand the red man and to present him fairly to others."—*New York Observer.*

IN PREPARATION.

The Story of the Mine. By CHARLES HOWARD SHINN.
The Story of the Trapper. By GILBERT PARKER.
The Story of the Explorer.
The Story of the Cowboy.
The Story of the Soldier.
The Story of the Railroad.

New York : D. APPLETON & CO., 72 Fifth Avenue.